A SHATTERING NOVEL
OF PAIN AND BETRAYAL!

A SEPARATE PEACE

"I think it is the best-written, best designed and most moving novel I have read in many years. Beginning with a tiny incident among ordinary boys, it ends by being as deep and as big as evil itself. As I read the story I had the feeling of climbing a tower and looking at wider and wider prospects of human nature, each bleaker than the last . . . The characters are real, the tragedy is inevitable, the setting is perfectly chosen. I shall recommend this book to anyone who tells me that the novel is no longer a work of art."

—Aubrey Menen

"A quietly vital and cleanly written novel
that moves, page by page,
toward a most interesting target."

—Truman Capote

ASK FOR LOVE AND THEY GIVE YOU RICE PUDDING
   by Bradford Angier and Barbara Corcoran
BLINDED BY THE LIGHT by Robin F. Brancato
CRAZY EIGHTS by Barbara Dana
DAVE'S SONG by Robert McKay
THE DOG DAYS OF ARTHUR CANE
   by T. Ernesto Bethancourt
DON'T SIT UNDER THE APPLE TREE
   by Robin F. Brancato
GENTLEHANDS by M. E. Kerr
GROWING ANYWAY UP by Florence Parry Heide
HOME BEFORE DARK by Sue Ellen Bridgers
NOBODY WAVED GOODBYE by Elizabeth Haggard
ONE FAT SUMMER by Robert Lipsyte
THE PIGMAN by Paul Zindel
THE PIGMAN'S LEGACY by Paul Zindel
QUEEN OF HEARTS by Vera and Bill Cleaver
A SEPARATE PEACE by John Knowles
SUMMER OF MY GERMAN SOLDIER by Bette Greene
TUNE IN YESTERDAY by T. Ernesto Bethancourt

A Separate Peace

by

John Knowles

BANTAM BOOKS
TORONTO · NEW YORK · LONDON · SYDNEY

RL 4, IL 6+

A SEPARATE PEACE

A Bantam Book / published by arrangement with
The Macmillan Company

PRINTING HISTORY

Macmillan edition published February 1960
A total of 11 printings

Bantam edition / February 1966
29 printings through June 1972
Bantam Pathfinder edition / October 1972
9 printings through April 1975
Bantam edition / October 1975

41st printing . November 1975	48th printing . . . . May 1979
42nd printing . . . March 1976	49th printing . November 1979
43rd printing . September 1976	50th printing . November 1979
44th printing . . . . . . July 1977	51st printing . . . . . June 1980
45th printing . . . . . May 1978	52nd printing . September 1980
46th printing . . . . . May 1978	53rd printing . . January 1981
47th printing . . . August 1978	54th printing . . October 1981

ISBN 0-553-20721-0

Published simultaneously in the United States and Canada

Bantam Books are published by Bantam Books, Inc. Its trade-
mark, consisting of the words "Bantam Books" and the por-
trayal of a rooster, is Registered in U.S. Patent and Trademark
Office and in other countries. Marca Registrada. Bantam
Books, Inc., 666 Fifth Avenue, New York, New York 10103.

PRINTED IN THE UNITED STATES OF AMERICA

63 62 61 60 59 58 57 56 55 54

To Bea and Jim
with gratitude and love

A SEPARATE PEACE

1

I went back to the Devon School not long ago, and found it looking oddly newer than when I was a student there fifteen years before. It seemed more sedate than I remembered it, more perpendicular and strait-laced, with narrower windows and shinier woodwork, as though a coat of varnish had been put over everything for better preservation. But, of course, fifteen years before there had been a war going on. Perhaps the school wasn't as well kept up in those days; perhaps varnish, along with everything else, had gone to war.

I didn't entirely like this glossy new surface, because it made the school look like a museum, and that's exactly what it was to me, and what I did not want it to be. In the deep, tacit way in which feeling becomes stronger than thought, I had always felt that the Devon School came into existence the day I entered it, was vibrantly real while I was a student there, and then blinked out like a candle the day I left.

Now here it was after all, preserved by some considerate hand with varnish and wax. Preserved along with it, like stale air in an unopened room, was the well known fear which had surrounded and filled those days, so much of it that I hadn't even known it was

there. Because, unfamiliar with the absence of fear
and what that was like, I had not been able to identify
its presence.

Looking back now across fifteen years, I could see
with great clarity the fear I had lived in, which must
mean that in the interval I had succeeded in a very
important undertaking: I must have made my escape
from it.

I felt fear's echo, and along with that I felt the un-
hinged, uncontrollable joy which had been its accom-
paniment and opposite face, joy which had broken out
sometimes in those days like Northern Lights across
black sky.

There were a couple of places now which I wanted
to see. Both were fearful sites, and that was why I
wanted to see them. So after lunch at the Devon Inn I
walked back toward the school. It was a raw, nondescript time of year, toward the end of November,
the kind of wet, self-pitying November day when
every speck of dirt stands out clearly. Devon luckily
had very little of such weather—the icy clamp of winter, or the radiant New Hampshire summers, were
more characteristic of it—but this day it blew wet,
moody gusts all around me.

I walked along Gilman Street, the best street in
town. The houses were as handsome and as unusual
as I remembered. Clever modernizations of old Colonial manses, extensions in Victorian wood, capacious
Greek Revival temples lined the street, as impressive
and just as forbidding as ever. I had rarely seen anyone go into one of them, or anyone playing on a lawn,
or even an open window. Today with their failing ivy
and stripped, moaning trees the houses looked both
more elegant and more lifeless than ever.

Like all old, good schools, Devon did not stand iso-

lated behind walls and gates but emerged naturally
from the town which had produced it. So there was
no sudden moment of encounter as I approached it;
the houses along Gilman Street began to look more
defensive, which meant that I was near the school,
and then more exhausted, which meant that I was
in it.

It was early afternoon and the grounds and buildings were deserted, since everyone was at sports.
There was nothing to distract me as I made my way
across a wide yard, called the Far Commons, and up
to a building as red brick and balanced as the other
major buildings, but with a large cupola and a bell
and a clock and Latin over the doorway—the First
Academy Building.

In through swinging doors I reached a marble foyer,
and stopped at the foot of a long white marble flight
of stairs. Although they were old stairs, the worn
moons in the middle of each step were not very deep.
The marble must be unusually hard. That seemed very
likely, only too likely, although with all my thought
about these stairs this exceptional hardness had not
occurred to me. It was surprising that I had overlooked that, that crucial fact.

There was nothing else to notice; they of course
were the same stairs I had walked up and down at
least once every day of my Devon life. They were the
same as ever. And I? Well, I naturally felt older—I
began at that point the emotional examination to note
how far my convalescence had gone—I was taller,
bigger generally in relation to these stairs. I had more
money and success and "security" than in the days
when specters seemed to go up and down them with
me.

I turned away and went back outside. The Far

Common was still empty, and I walked alone down
the wide gravel paths among those most Republican,
bankerish of trees, New England elms, toward the far
side of the school.

Devon is sometimes considered the most beautiful
school in New England, and even on this dismal afternoon its power was asserted. It is the beauty of small
areas of order—a large yard, a group of trees, three
similar dormitories, a circle of old houses—living together in contentious harmony. You felt that an argument might begin again any time; in fact it had: out
of the Dean's Residence, a pure and authentic Colonial house, there now sprouted an ell with a big bare
picture window. Some day the Dean would probably
live entirely encased in a house of glass and be happy
as a sandpiper. Everything at Devon slowly changed
and slowly harmonized with what had gone before. So
it was logical to hope that since the buildings and the
Deans and the curriculum could achieve this, I could
achieve, perhaps unknowingly already had achieved,
this growth and harmony myself.

I would know more about that when I had seen the
second place I had come to see. So I roamed on past
the balanced red brick dormitories with webs of leaf-
less ivy clinging to them, through a ramshackle salient
of the town which invaded the school for a hundred
yards, past the solid gymnasium, full of students at
this hour but silent as a monument on the outside,
past the Field House, called The Cage—I remembered
now what a mystery references to "The Cage" had
been during my first weeks at Devon, I had thought
it must be a place of severe punishment—and I
reached the huge open sweep of ground known as the
Playing Fields.

Devon was both scholarly and very athletic, so the

playing fields were vast and, except at such a time of year, constantly in use. Now they reached soggily and emptily away from me, forlorn tennis courts on the left, enormous football and soccer and lacrosse fields in the center, woods on the right, and at the far end a small river detectable from this distance by the few bare trees along its banks. It was such a gray and misty day that I could not see the other side of the river, where there was a small stadium.

I started the long trudge across the fields and had gone some distance before I paid any attention to the soft and muddy ground, which was dooming my city shoes. I didn't stop. Near the center of the fields there were thin lakes of muddy water which I had to make my way around, my unrecognizable shoes making obscene noises as I lifted them out of the mire. With nothing to block it the wind flung wet gusts at me; at any other time I would have felt like a fool slogging through mud and rain, only to look at a tree.

A little fog hung over the river so that as I neared it I felt myself becoming isolated from everything except the river and the few trees beside it. The wind was blowing more steadily here, and I was beginning to feel cold. I never wore a hat, and had forgotten gloves. There were several trees bleakly reaching into the fog. Any one of them might have been the one I was looking for. Unbelievable that there were other trees which looked like it here. It had loomed in my memory as a huge lone spike dominating the river-bank, forbidding as an artillery piece, high as the beanstalk. Yet here was a scattered grove of trees, none of them of any particular grandeur.

Moving through the soaked, coarse grass I began to examine each one closely, and finally identified the tree I was looking for by means of certain small scars

rising along its trunk, and by a limb extending over
the river, and another thinner limb growing near it.
This was the tree, and it seemed to me standing there
to resemble those men, the giants of your childhood,
whom you encounter years later and find that they are
not merely smaller in relation to your growth, but
that they are absolutely smaller, shrunken by age. In
this double demotion the old giants have become pig-
mies while you were looking the other way.

The tree was not only stripped by the cold season, it
seemed weary from age, enfeebled, dry. I was thankful, very thankful that I had seen it. So the more
things remain the same, the more they change after all
—*plus c'est la même chose, plus ça change.* Nothing
endures, not a tree, not love, not even a death by
violence.

Changed, I headed back through the mud. I was
drenched; anybody could see it was time to come in
out of the rain. X X X X X

Flashback

The tree was tremendous, an irate, steely black
steeple beside the river. I was damned if I'd climb it.
The hell with it. No one but Phineas could think up
such a crazy idea.

He of course saw nothing the slightest bit intimi-
dating about it. He wouldn't, or wouldn't admit it if
he did. Not Phineas.

"What I like best about this tree," he said in that
voice of his, the equivalent in sound of a hypnotist's
eyes, "what I like is that it's such a cinch!" He opened
his green eyes wider and gave us his maniac look, and
only the smirk on his wide mouth with its droll,
slightly protruding upper lip reassured us that he
wasn't completely goofy.

"Is that what you like best?" I said sarcastically. I

said a lot of things sarcastically that summer; that was my sarcastic summer, 1942.

"Aey-uh," he said. This weird New England affirmative—maybe it is spelled "aie-huh"—always made me laugh, as Finny knew, so I had to laugh, which made me feel less sarcastic and less scared.

There were three others with us—Phineas in those days almost always moved in groups the size of a hockey team—and they stood with me looking with masked apprehension from him to the tree. Its soaring black trunk was set with rough wooden pegs leading up to a substantial limb which extended farther toward the water. Standing on this limb, you could by a prodigious effort jump far enough out into the river for safety. So we had heard. At least the seventeen-year-old bunch could do it; but they had a crucial year's advantage over us. No Upper Middler, which was the name for our class in the Devon School, had ever tried. Naturally Finny was going to be the first to try, and just as naturally he was going to inveigle others, us, into trying it with him.

We were not even Upper Middler exactly. For this was the Summer Session, just established to keep up with the pace of the war. We were in shaky transit that summer from the groveling status of Lower Middlers to the near-respectability of Upper Middlers. The class above, seniors, draft-bait, practically soldiers, rushed ahead of us toward the war. They were caught up in accelerated courses and first-aid programs and a physical hardening regimen, which included jumping from this tree. We were still calmly, numbly reading Virgil and playing tag in the river farther downstream. Until Finny thought of the tree.

We stood looking up at it, four looks of consternation, one of excitement. "Do you want to go first?"

Finny asked us, rhetorically. We just looked quietly
back at him, and so he began taking off his clothes,
stripping down to his underpants. For such an extraordinary athlete—even as a Lower Middler Phineas had
been the best athlete in the school—he was not spec-
tacularly built. He was my height—five feet eight and
a half inches (I had been claiming five feet nine
inches before he became my roommate, but he had
said in public with that simple, shocking self-accept-
ance of his, "No, you're the same height I am, five-
eight and a half. We're on the short side"). He
weighed a hundred and fifty pounds, a galling ten
pounds more than I did, which flowed from his legs to
torso around shoulders to arms and full strong neck in
an uninterrupted, unemphatic unity of strength.

He began scrambling up the wooden pegs nailed to
the side of the tree, his back muscles working like a
panther's. The pegs didn't seem strong enough to hold
his weight. At last he stepped onto the branch which
reached a little farther toward the water. "Is this the
one they jump from?" None of us knew. "If I do it,
you're all going to do it, aren't you?" We didn't say
anything very clearly. "Well," he cried out, "here's my
contribution to the war effort!" and he sprang out, fell
through the tops of some lower branches, and smashed
into the water.

"Great!" he said, bobbing instantly to the surface
again, his wet hair plastered in droll bangs on his
forehead. "That's the most fun I've had this week.
Who's next?"

I was. This tree flooded me with a sensation of
alarm all the way to my tingling fingers. My head began to feel unnaturally light, and the vague rustling
sounds from the nearby woods came to me as though

muffled and filtered. I must have been entering a mild state of shock. Insulated by this, I took off my clothes and started to climb the pegs. I don't remember saying anything. The branch he had jumped from was slenderer than it looked from the ground and much higher. It was impossible to walk out on it far enough to be well over the river. I would have to spring far out or risk falling into the shallow water next to the bank. "Come on," drawled Finny from below, "stop standing there showing off." I recognized with automatic tenseness that the view was very impressive from here. "When they torpedo the troopship," he shouted, "you can't stand around admiring the view. Jump!"

What was I doing up here anyway? Why did I let Finny talk me into stupid things like this? Was he getting some kind of hold over me?

"Jump!"

With the sensation that I was throwing my life away, I jumped into space. Some tips of branches snapped past me and then I crashed into the water. My legs hit the soft mud of the bottom, and immediately I was on the surface being congratulated. I felt fine.

"I think that was better than Finny's," said Elwin —better known as Leper—Lepellier, who was bidding for an ally in the dispute he foresaw.

"All right, pal," Finny spoke in his cordial, penetrating voice, that reverberant instrument in his chest, "don't start awarding prizes until you've passed the course. The tree is waiting."

Leper closed his mouth as though forever. He didn't argue or refuse. He didn't back away. He became inanimate. But the other two, Chet Douglass and Bobby

Zane, were vocal enough, complaining shrilly about school regulations, the danger of stomach cramps, physical disabilities they had never mentioned before.

"It's you, pal," Finny said to me at last, "just you and me." He and I started back across the fields, preceding the others like two seigneurs.

We were the best of friends at that moment.

"You were very good," said Finny good-humoredly, "once I shamed you into it."

"You didn't shame anybody into anything."

"Oh yes I did. I'm good for you that way. You have a tendency to back away from things otherwise."

"I never backed away from anything in my life!" I cried, my indignation at this charge naturally stronger because it was so true. "You're goofy!"

Phineas just walked serenely on, or rather flowed on, rolling forward in his white sneakers with such unthinking unity of movement that "walk" didn't describe it.

I went along beside him across the enormous playing fields toward the gym. Underfoot the healthy green turf was brushed with dew, and ahead of us we could see a faint green haze hanging above the grass, shot through with the twilight sun. Phineas stopped talking for once, so that now I could hear cricket noises and bird cries of dusk, a gymnasium truck gunning along an empty athletic road a quarter of a mile away, a burst of faint, isolated laughter carried to us from the back door of the gym, and then over all, cool and matriarchal, the six o'clock bell from the Academy Building cupola, the calmest, most carrying bell toll in the world, civilized, calm, invincible, and final.

The toll sailed over the expansive tops of all the elms, the great slanting roofs and formidable chimneys of the dormitories, the narrow and brittle old house-

tops, across the open New Hampshire sky to us coming back from the river. "We'd better hurry or we'll
be late for dinner," I said, breaking into what Finny
called my "West Point stride." Phineas didn't really
dislike West Point in particular or authority in general, but just considered authority the necessary evil
against which happiness was achieved by reaction,
the backboard which returned all the insults he threw
at it. My "West Point stride" was intolerable; his right
foot flashed into the middle of my fast walk and I
went pitching forward into the grass. "Get those hundred and fifty pounds off me!" I shouted, because he
was sitting on my back. Finny got up, patted my head
genially, and moved on across the field, not deigning
to glance around for my counterattack, but relying on
his extrasensory ears, his ability to feel in the air
someone coming on him from behind. As I sprang at
him he side-stepped easily, but I just managed to kick
him as I shot past. He caught my leg and there was a
brief wrestling match on the turf which he won. "Better hurry," he said, "or they'll put you in the guard-
house." We were walking again, faster; Bobby and
Leper and Chet were urging us from ahead for God's
sake to hurry up, and then Finny trapped me again
in his strongest trap, that is, I suddenly became his
collaborator. As we walked rapidly along I abruptly
resented the bell and my West Point stride and hurrying and conforming. Finny was right. And there was
only one way to show him this. I threw my hip against
his, catching him by surprise, and he was instantly
down, definitely pleased. This was why he liked me
so much. When I jumped on top of him, my knees on
his chest, he couldn't ask for anything better. We
struggled in some equality for a while, and then when
we were sure we were too late for dinner, we broke off.

He and I passed the gym and came on toward the first group of dormitories, which were dark and silent. There were only two hundred of us at Devon in the summer, not enough to fill most of the school. We passed the sprawling Headmaster's house—empty, he was doing something for the government in Washington; past the Chapel—empty again, used only for a short time in the mornings; past the First Academy Building, where there were some dim lights shining from a few of its many windows, Masters at work in their classrooms there; down a short slope into the broad and well clipped Common, on which light fell from the big surrounding Georgian buildings. A dozen boys were loafing there on the grass after dinner, and a kitchen rattle from the wing of one of the buildings accompanied their talk. The sky was darkening steadily, which brought up the lights in the dormitories and the old houses; a loud phonograph a long way off played *Don't Sit Under the Apple Tree,* rejected that and played *They're Either Too Young or Too Old,* grew more ambitious with *The Warsaw Concerto,* mellower with *The Nutcracker Suite,* and then stopped.

Finny and I went to our room. Under the yellow study lights we read our Hardy assignments; I was halfway through *Tess of the D'Urbervilles,* he carried on his baffled struggle with *Far from the Madding Crowd,* amused that there should be people named Gabriel Oak and Bathsheba Everdene. Our illegal radio, turned too low to be intelligible, was broadcasting the news. Outside there was a rustling early summer movement of the wind; the seniors, allowed out later than we were, came fairly quietly back as the bell sounded ten stately times. Boys ambled past our door toward the bathroom, and there was a period of steadily pouring shower water. Then lights began to snap out all over the school. We undressed, and I put on some pajamas, but Phineas, who had heard they were unmilitary, didn't; there was the silence in which it was understood we were saying some prayers, and then that summer school day came to an end.

2

Our absence from dinner had been noticed. The following morning—the clean-washed shine of summer mornings in the north country—Mr. Prud'homme stopped at our door. He was broad-shouldered, grave, and he wore a gray business suit. He did not have the careless, almost British look of most of the Devon Masters, because he was a substitute for the summer. He enforced such rules as he knew; missing dinner was one of them.

We had been swimming in the river, Finny explained; then there had been a wrestling match, then there was that sunset that anybody would want to watch, then there'd been several friends we had to see on business—he rambled on, his voice soaring and plunging in its vibrant sound box, his eyes now and then widening to fire a flash of green across the room. Standing in the shadows, with the bright window behind him, he blazed with sunburned health. As Mr. Prud'homme looked at him and listened to the scatterbrained eloquence of his explanation, he could be seen rapidly losing his grip on sternness.

"If you hadn't already missed nine meals in the last two weeks . . ." he broke in.

But Finny pressed his advantage. Not because he

wanted to be forgiven for missing the meal—that didn't interest him at all, he might have rather enjoyed the punishment if it was done in some novel and unknown way. He pressed his advantage because he saw that Mr. Prud'homme was pleased, won over in spite of himself. The Master was slipping from his official position momentarily, and it was just possible, if Phineas pressed hard enough, that there might be a flow of simple, unregulated friendliness between them, and such flows were one of Finny's reasons for living.

"The real reason, sir, was that we just had to jump out of that tree. You know that tree . . ." I knew, Mr. Prud'homme must have known, Finny knew, if he stopped to think, that jumping out of the tree was even more forbidden than missing a meal. "We had to do that, naturally," he went on, "because we're all getting ready for the war. What if they lower the draft age to seventeen? Gene and I are both going to be seventeen at the end of the summer, which is a very convenient time since it's the start of the academic year and there's never any doubt about which class you should be in. Leper Lepellier is already seventeen, and if I'm not mistaken he will be draftable before the end of this next academic year, and so conceivably he ought to have been in the class ahead, he ought to have been a senior now, if you see what I mean, so that he would have been graduated and been all set to be drafted. But we're all right, Gene and I are perfectly all right. There isn't any question that we are conforming in every possible way to everything that's happening and everything that's going to happen. It's all a question of birthdays, unless you want to be more specific and look at it from the sexual point of view, which I have never cared to do myself, since it's a question of my mother and my father, and I have never felt I wanted to think about their sexual lives too much." Everything he said was true and sincere; Finny always said what he happened to be thinking, and if this stunned people then he was surprised.

Mr. Prud'homme released his breath with a sort of amazed laugh, stared at Finny for a while, and that was all there was to it.

This was the way the Masters tended to treat us that summer. They seemed to be modifying their usual attitude of floating, chronic disapproval. During the winter most of them regarded anything unexpected in a student with suspicion, seeming to feel that anything we said or did was potentially illegal. Now on these clear June days in New Hampshire they appeared to uncoil, they seemed to believe that we were with them about half the time, and only spent the other half trying to make fools of them. A streak of tolerance was detectable; Finny decided that they were beginning to show commendable signs of maturity.

It was partly his doing. The Devon faculty had never before experienced a student who combined a calm ignorance of the rules with a winning urge to be good, who seemed to love the school truly and deeply, and never more than when he was breaking the regulations, a model boy who was most comfortable in the truant's corner. The faculty threw up its hands over Phineas, and so loosened its grip on all of us.

But there was another reason. I think we reminded them of what peace was like, we boys of sixteen. We were registered with no draft board, we had taken no physical examinations. No one had ever tested us for hernia or color blindness. Trick knees and punctured eardrums were minor complaints and not yet disabilities which would separate a few from the fate of the rest. We were careless and wild, and I suppose we could be thought of as a sign of the life the war was being fought to preserve. Anyway, they were more indulgent toward us than at any other time; they snapped at the heels of the seniors, driving and molding and arming them for the war. They noticed our games tolerantly. We reminded them of what peace was like, of lives which were not bound up with destruction.

Phineas was the essence of this careless peace. Not that he was unconcerned about the war. After Mr. Prud'homme left he began to dress, that is he began reaching for whatever clothes were nearest, some of them mine. Then he stopped to consider, and went over to the dresser. Out of one of the drawers he lifted a finely woven broadcloth shirt, carefully cut, and very pink.

"What's *that* thing?"

"This is a tablecloth," he said out of the side of his mouth.

"No, cut it out. What is it?"

"This," he then answered with some pride, "is going to be my emblem. Ma sent it up last week. Did you ever see stuff like this, and a color like this? It doesn't even button all the way down. You have to pull it over your head, like this."

"Over your head? Pink! It makes you look like a *fairy!*"

"Does it?" He used this preoccupied tone when he was thinking of something more interesting than what you had said. But his mind always recorded what was said and played it back to him when there was time, so as he was buttoning the high collar in front of the mirror he said mildly, "I wonder what would happen if I looked like a fairy to everyone."

"You're nuts."

"Well, in case suitors begin clamoring at the door, you can tell them I'm wearing this as an emblem." He turned around to let me admire it. "I was reading in the paper that we bombed Central Europe for the first time the other day." Only someone who knew Phineas as well as I did could realize that he was not changing the subject. I waited quietly for him to make whatever fantastic connection there might be between this and his shirt. "Well, we've got to do something to *celebrate*. We haven't got a flag, we can't float Old Glory proudly out the window. So I'm going to wear this, as an emblem."

He did wear it. No one else in the school could have done so without some risk of having it torn from his back. When the sternest of the Summer Sessions Masters, old Mr. Patch-Withers, came up to him after history class and asked about it, I watched his drawn but pink face become pinker with amusement as Finny politely explained the meaning of the shirt.

It was hypnotism. I was beginning to see that Phineas could get away with anything. I couldn't help envying him that a little, which was perfectly normal. There was no harm in envying even your best friend a little.

In the afternoon Mr. Patch-Withers, who was substitute Headmaster for the summer, offered the traditional term tea to the Upper Middle class. It was held in the deserted Headmaster's house, and Mr. Patch-Withers' wife trembled at every cup tinkle. We were in a kind of sun porch and conservatory combined, spacious and damp and without many plants. Those there were had large nonflowering stalks, with big barbaric leaves. The chocolate brown wicker furniture shot out menacing twigs, and three dozen of us stood tensely teetering our cups amid the wicker and leaves, trying hard not to sound as inane in our conversation with the four present Masters and their wives as they sounded to us.

Phineas had soaked and brushed his hair for the occasion. This gave his head a sleek look, which was contradicted by the surprised, honest expression which he wore on his face. His ears, I had never noticed before, were fairly small and set close to his head, and combined with his plastered hair they now gave his bold nose and cheekbones the sharp look of a prow.

He alone talked easily. He discussed the bombing of Central Europe. No one else happened to have seen the story, and since Phineas could not recall exactly what target in which country had been hit, or whether it was the American, British, or even Russian air force which had hit it, or what day he read it in which newspaper, the discussion was one-sided.

That didn't matter. It was the event which counted. But after a while Finny felt he should carry the discussion to others. "I think we ought to bomb the daylights out of them, as long as we don't hit any women or children or old people, don't you?" he was saying to Mrs. Patch-Withers, perched nervously behind her urn. "Or hospitals," he went on. "And naturally no schools. Or churches."

"We must also be careful about works of art," she put in, "if they are of permanent value."

".A lot of nonsense," Mr. Patch-Withers grumbled, with a flushed face. "How do you expect our boys to be as precise as that thousands of feet up with bombs weighing tons! Look at what the Germans did to Amsterdam! Look at what they did to Coventry!"

"The Germans aren't the Central Europeans, dear," his wife said very gently.

He didn't like being brought up short. But he seemed to be just able to bear it, from his wife. After a temperamental pause he said gruffly, "There isn't any 'permanent art' in Central Europe anyway."

Finny was enjoying this. He unbuttoned his seersucker jacket, as though he needed greater body freedom for the discussion. Mrs. Patch-Withers' glance then happened to fall on his belt. In a tentative voice she said, "Isn't that the . . . our . . ." Her husband looked; I panicked. In his haste that morning Finny had not unexpectedly used a tie for a belt. But this morning the first tie at hand had been the Devon School tie.

This time he wasn't going to get away with it. I could feel myself becoming unexpectedly excited at that. Mr. Patch-Withers' face was reaching a brilliant shade, and his wife's head fell as though before the guillotine. Even Finny seemed to color a little, unless it was the reflection from his pink shirt. But his expression was composed, and he said in his resonant voice, "I wore this, you see, because it goes with the shirt and it all ties in together—I didn't mean that to be a pun, I don't think they're very funny, especially in polite company, do you?—it all ties in together with what we've been talking about, this bombing in Central Europe, because when you come right down to it the school is involved in everything that happens in the war, it's all the same war and the same world, and I think Devon ought to be included. I don't know whether you think the way I do on that."

Mr. Patch-Withers' face had been shifting expressions and changing colors continuously, and now it settled into fixed surprise. "I never heard anything so illogical as that in my life!" He didn't sound very indignant, though. "That's probably the strangest tribute this school has had in a hundred and sixty years." He seemed pleased or amused in some unknown corner of his mind. Phineas was going to get away with even this.

His eyes gave their wider, magical gleam and his voice continued on a more compelling level, "Although I have to admit I didn't think of that when I put it on this morning." He smiled pleasantly after supplying this interesting additional information. Mr. Patch-Withers settled into a hearty silence at this, and so Finny added, "I'm glad I put on *something* for a belt! I certainly would hate the embarrassment of having my pants fall down at the Headmaster's tea. Of course he isn't here. But it would be just as embarrassing in front of you and Mrs. Patch-Withers," and he smiled politely down at her.

Mr. Patch-Withers' laughter surprised us all, including himself. His face, whose shades we had often labeled, now achieved a new one. Phineas was very happy; sour and stern Mr. Patch-Withers had been given a good laugh for once, and he had done it! He broke into the charmed, thoughtless grin of a man fulfilled.

He had gotten away with everything. I felt a sudden stab of disappointment. That was because I just wanted to see some more excitement; that must have been it.

We left the party, both of us feeling fine. I laughed along with Finny, my best friend, and also unique, able to get away with anything at all. And not because he was a conniver either; I was sure of that. He got away with everything because of the extraordinary kind of person he was. It was quite a compliment to me, as a matter of fact, to have such a person choose me for his best friend.

Finny never left anything alone, not when it was well enough, not when it was perfect. "Let's go jump in the river," he said under his breath as we went out of the sun porch. He forced compliance by leaning against me as we walked along, changing my direction; like a police car squeezing me to the side of the road, he directed me unwillingly toward the gym and the river. "We need to clear our heads of that party," he said, "all that talk!"

"Yes. It sure was boring. Who did most of the talking anyway?"

Finny concentrated. "Mr. Patch-Withers was pretty gassy, and his wife, and . . ."

"Yeah. And?"

Turning a look of mock shock on me, "You don't mean to infer that *I* talked too much!"

Returning, with interest, his gaping shock, "You? Talk too much? How can you accuse me of accusing you of that!" As I said, this was my sarcastic summer. It was only long after that I recognized sarcasm as the protest of people who are weak.

We walked along through the shining afternoon to the river. "I don't really believe we bombed Central Europe, do you?" said Finny thoughtfully. The dormitories we passed were massive and almost anonymous behind their thick layers of ivy, big, old-looking leaves you would have thought stayed there winter and summer, permanent hanging gardens in New Hampshire. Between the buildings, elms curved so high that you ceased to remember their height until you looked above the familiar trunks and the lowest umbrellas of leaves and took in the lofty complex they held high above, branches and branches of branches, a world of branches with an infinity of leaves. They too seemed permanent and never-changing, an untouched, unreachable world high in space, like the ornamental towers and spires of a great church, too high to be enjoyed, too high for anything, great and remote and never useful. "No, I don't think I believe it either," I answered.

Far ahead of us four boys, looking like white flags on the endless green playing fields, crossed toward the tennis courts. To the right of them the gym meditated behind its gray walls, the high, wide, oval-topped windows shining back at the sun. Beyond the gym and the fields began the woods, our, the Devon School's woods, which in my imagination were the beginning of the great northern forests. I thought that, from the Devon Woods, trees reached in an unbroken, widening corridor so far to the north that no one had ever seen the other end, somewhere up in the far unorganized tips of Canada. We seemed to be playing on the tame fringe of the last and greatest wilderness. I never found out whether this is so and perhaps it is.

Bombs in Central Europe were completely unreal to us here, not because we couldn't imagine it—a thousand newspaper photographs and newsreels had given us a pretty accurate idea of such a sight—but because our place here was too fair for us to accept something like that. We spent that summer in complete selfishness, I'm happy to say. The people in the world who could be selfish in the summer of 1942 were a small band, and I'm glad we took advantage of it.

"The first person who says anything unpleasant will get a swift kick in the ass," said Finny reflectively as we came to the river.

"All right."

"Are you still afraid to jump out of the tree?"

"There's something unpleasant about that question, isn't there?"

"That question? No, of course not. It depends on how you answer it."

"Afraid to jump out of that tree? I expect it'll be a very pleasant jump."

After we had swum around in the water for a while Finny said, "Will you do me the pleasure of jumping out of the tree first?"

"My pleasure."

Rigid, I began climbing the rungs, slightly reassured by having Finny right behind me. "We'll jump together to cement our partnership," he said. "We'll form a suicide society, and the membership requirement is one jump out of this tree."

"A suicide society," I said stiffly. "The Suicide Society of the Summer Session."

"Good! The *Super* Suicide Society of the Summer Session! How's that?"

"That's fine, that's okay."

We were standing on a limb, I a little farther out than Finny. I turned to say something else, some stalling remark, something to delay even a few seconds more, and then I realized that in turning I had begun to lose my balance. There was a moment of total, impersonal panic, and then Finny's hand shot out and grabbed my arm, and with my balance restored, the panic immediately disappeared. I turned back toward the river, moved a few more steps along the limb, sprang far out and fell into the deep water. Finny also made a good jump, and the Super Suicide Society of the Summer Session was officially established.

It was only after dinner, when I was on my way alone to the library, that the full danger I had brushed on the limb shook me again. If Finny hadn't come up right behind me . . . if he hadn't been there . . . I could have fallen on the bank and broken my back! if I had fallen awkwardly enough I could have been killed. Finny had practically saved my life.

3

Yes, he had practically saved my life. He had also practically lost it for me. I wouldn't have been on that damn limb except for him. I wouldn't have turned around, and so lost my balance, if he hadn't been there. I didn't need to feel any tremendous rush of gratitude toward Phineas.

The Super Suicide Society of the Summer Session was a success from the start. That night Finny began to talk abstractedly about it, as though it were a venerable, entrenched institution of the Devon School. The half-dozen friends who were there in our room listening began to bring up small questions on details without ever quite saying that they had never heard of such a club. Schools are supposed to be catacombed with secret societies and underground brotherhoods, and as far as they knew here was one which had just come to the surface. They signed up as "trainees" on the spot.

We began to meet every night to initiate them. The Charter Members, he and I, had to open every meeting by jumping ourselves. This was the first of the many rules which Finny created without notice during the summer. I hated it. I never got inured to the jumping. At every meeting the limb seemed higher, thinner, the deeper water harder to reach. Every time, when I got myself into position to jump, I felt a flash of disbelief that I was doing anything so perilous. But I always jumped. Otherwise I would have lost face with Phineas, and that would have been unthinkable.

We met every night, because Finny's life was ruled by inspiration and anarchy, and so he prized a set of rules. His own, not those imposed on him by other people, such as the faculty of the Devon School. The Super Suicide Society of the Summer Session was a club; clubs by definition met regularly; we met every night. Nothing could be more regular than that. To meet once a week seemed to him much less regular, entirely too haphazard, bordering on carelessness.

I went along; I never missed a meeting. At that time it would never have occurred to me to say, "I don't feel like it tonight," which was the plain truth every night. I was subject to the dictates of my mind, which gave me the maneuverability of a strait jacket. "We're off, pal," Finny would call out, and acting against every instinct of my nature, I went without a thought of protest.

As we drifted on through the summer, with this one inflexible appointment every day—classes could be cut, meals missed, Chapel skipped—I noticed something about Finny's own mind, which was such an opposite from mine. It wasn't completely unleashed after all. I noticed that he did abide by certain rules, which he seemed to cast in the form of Commandments. "Never say you are five feet nine when you are five feet eight and a half" was the first one I encountered. Another was, "Always say some prayers at night because it might turn out that there is a God."

But the one which had the most urgent influence in his life was, "You always win at sports." This "you" was collective. Everyone always won at sports. When you played a game you won, in the same way as when you sat down to a meal you ate it. It inevitably and naturally followed. Finny never permitted himself to realize that when you won they lost. That would have destroyed the perfect beauty which was sport. Nothing bad ever happened in sports; they were the absolute good.

He was disgusted with that summer's athletic program—a little tennis, some swimming, clumsy softball games, badminton. "Badminton!" he exploded the day it entered the schedule. He said nothing else, but the shocked, outraged, despairing note of anguish in the word said all the rest. "*Badminton!*"

"At least it's not as bad as the seniors," I said, handing him the fragile racquet and the fey shuttlecock. "They're doing calisthenics."

"What are they trying to do?" He swatted the shuttlecock the length of the locker room. "Destroy us?" Humor infiltrated the outrage in his voice, which meant that he was thinking of a way out.

We went outside into the cordial afternoon sunshine. The playing fields were optimistically green and empty before us. The tennis courts were full. The softball diamond was busy. A pattern of badminton nets swayed sensually in the breeze. Finny eyed them with quiet astonishment. Far down the fields toward the river there was a wooden tower about ten feet high where the instructor had stood to direct the senior calisthenics. It was empty now. The seniors had been trotted off to the improvised obstacle course in the woods, or to have their blood pressure taken again, or to undergo an insidious exercise in The Cage which consisted in stepping up on a box and down again in rapid rhythm for five minutes. They were off somewhere, shaping up for the war. All of the fields were ours.

Finny began to walk slowly in the direction of the tower. Perhaps he was thinking that we might carry it the rest of the way to the river and throw it in; perhaps he was just interested in looking at it, as he was in everything. Whatever he thought, he forgot it when we reached the tower. Beside it someone had left a large and heavy leather-covered ball, a medicine ball.

He picked it up. "Now this, you see, is everything in the world you need for sports. When they discovered the circle they created sports. As for this thing," embracing the medicine ball in his left arm he held up the shuttlecock, contaminated, in his outstretched right, "this idiot tickler, the only thing it's good for is eeny-meeny-miney-mo." He dropped the ball and proceeded to pick the feathers out of the shuttlecock, distastefully, as though removing ticks from a dog. The remaining rubber plug he then threw out of sight down the field, with a single lunge ending in a powerful downward thrust of his wrist. Badminton was gone.

He stood balancing the medicine ball, enjoying the feel of it. "All you really need is a round ball."

Although he was rarely conscious of it, Phineas was always being watched, like the weather. Up the field the others at badminton sensed a shift in the wind; their voices carried down to us, calling us. When we didn't come, they began gradually to come down to us.

"I think it's about time we started to get a little *exercise* around here, don't you?" he said, cocking his head at me. Then he slowly looked around at the others with the expression of dazed determination he used when the object was to carry people along with his latest idea. He blinked twice, and then said, "We can always start with this ball."

"Let's make it have something to do with the war," suggested Bobby Zane. "Like a blitzkrieg or something."

"Blitzkrieg," repeated Finny doubtfully.

"We could figure out some kind of blitzkrieg baseball," I said.

"We'll call it blitzkrieg ball," said Bobby.

"Or just blitzball," reflected Finny. "Yes, blitzball." Then, with an expectant glance around, "Well, let's get started," he threw the big, heavy ball at me. I grasped it against my chest with both arms. "Well, run!" ordered Finny. "No, not *that* way! Toward the river! Run!" I headed toward the river surrounded by the others in a hesitant herd; they sensed that in all probability they were my adversaries in blitzball. "Don't hog it!" Finny yelled. "Throw it to somebody else. Otherwise, naturally," he talked steadily as he ran along beside me, "now that we've got you surrounded, one of us will knock you down."

"Do what!" I veered away from him, hanging on to the clumsy ball. "What kind of a game is that?"

"Blitzball!" Chet Douglass shouted, throwing himself around my legs, knocking me down.

"That naturally was completely illegal," said Finny. "You don't use your *arms* when you knock the ball carrier down."

"You don't?" mumbled Chet from on top of me.

"No. You keep your arms crossed like this on your chest, and you just butt the ball carrier. No elbowing allowed either. All right, Gene, start again."

I began quickly, "Wouldn't somebody else have possession of the ball after—"

"Not when you've been knocked down illegally. The ball carrier retains possession in a case like that. So it's perfectly okay, you still have the ball. Go ahead."

There was nothing to do but start running again, with the others trampling with stronger will around me. "Throw it!" ordered Phineas. Bobby Zane was more or less in the clear and so I threw it at him; it was so heavy that he had to scoop my throw up from the ground. "Perfectly okay," commented Finny, running forward at top speed, "perfectly okay for the ball to touch the ground when it is being passed." Bobby doubled back closer to me for protection. "Knock him down," Finny yelled at me.

"Knock him down! Are you crazy? He's on my team!"

"There aren't any teams in blitzball," he yelled somewhat irritably, "we're all enemies. Knock him down!"

I knocked him down. "All right," said Finny as he disentangled us. "Now you have possession again." He handed the leaden ball to me.

"I would have thought that possession passed—"

"Naturally you gained possession of the ball when you knocked him down. Run."

So I began running again. Leper Lepellier was loping along outside my perimeter, not noticing the game, taggling along without reason, like a porpoise escorting a passing ship. "Leper!" I threw the ball past a few heads at him.

Taken by surprise, Leper looked up in anguish, shrank away from the ball, and voiced his first thought, a typical one. "I don't want it!"

"Stop, stop!" cried Finny in a referee's tone. Everybody halted, and Finny retrieved the ball; he talked better holding it. "Now Leper has just brought out a really important fine point of the game. The receiver can *refuse* a pass if he happens to choose to. Since we're all enemies, we can and will turn on each other all the time. We call that the Lepellier Refusal." We all nodded without speaking. "Here, Gene, the ball is of course still yours."

"Still mine? Nobody else has had the ball but me, for God sakes!"

"They'll get their chance. Now if you are refused three times in the course of running from the tower to the river, you go all the way back to the tower and start over. Naturally."

Blitzball was the surprise of the summer. Everybody played it; I believe a form of it is still popular at Devon. But nobody can be playing it as it was played by Phineas. He had unconsciously invented a game which brought his own athletic gifts to their highest pitch. The odds were tremendously against the ball carrier, so that Phineas was driven to exceed himself practically every day when he carried the ball. To escape the wolf pack which all the other players became he created reverses and deceptions and acts of sheer mass hypnotism which were so extraordinary that they surprised even him; after some of these plays I would notice him chuckling quietly to himself, in a kind of happy disbelief. In such a nonstop game he also had the natural advantage of a flow of energy which I never saw interrupted. I never saw him tired, never really winded, never overcharged and never restless. At dawn, all day long, and at midnight, Phineas always had a steady and formidable flow of usable energy.

Right from the start, it was clear that no one had ever been better adapted to a sport than Finny was to blitzball. I saw that right away. Why not? He had made it up, hadn't he? It needn't be surprising that he was sensationally good at it, and that the rest of us were more or less bumblers in our different ways. I suppose it served us right for letting him do all the planning. I didn't really think about it myself. What difference did it make? It was just a game. It was good that Finny could shine at it. He could also shine at many other things, with people for instance, the others in our dormitory, the faculty; in fact, if you stopped to think about it, Finny could shine with everyone, he attracted everyone he met. I was glad of that too. Naturally. He was my roommate and my best friend.

Everyone has a moment in history which belongs particularly to him. It is the moment when his emotions achieve their most powerful sway over him, and afterward when you say to this person "the world today" or "life" or "reality" he will assume that you mean this moment, even if it is fifty years past. The world, through his unleashed emotions, imprinted itself upon him, and he carries the stamp of that passing moment forever.

For me, this moment—four years is a moment in history—was the war. The war was and is reality for me. I still instinctively live and think in its atmosphere. These are some of its characteristics: Franklin Delano Roosevelt is the President of the United States, and he always has been. The other two eternal world leaders are Winston Churchill and Josef Stalin. America is not, never has been, and never will be what the songs and poems call it, a land of plenty. Nylon, meat, gasoline, and steel are rare. There are too many jobs and not enough workers. Money is very easy to earn but rather hard to spend, because there isn't very much to buy. Trains are always late and always crowded with "servicemen." The war will always be fought very far from America and it will never end. Nothing in America stands still for very long, including the people, who are always either leaving or on leave. People in America cry often. Sixteen is the key and crucial and natural age for a human being to be, and people of all other ages are ranged in an orderly manner ahead of and behind you as a harmonious setting for the sixteen-year-olds of this world. When you are sixteen, adults are slightly impressed and almost intimidated by you. This is a puzzle, finally solved by the realization that they foresee your military future, fighting for them. You do not foresee it. To waste anything in America is immoral. String and tinfoil are treasures. Newspapers are always crowded with strange maps and names of towns, and every few months the earth seems to lurch from its path when you see something in the newspapers, such as the time Mussolini, who had almost seemed one of the eternal leaders, is photographed hanging upside down on a meathook. Everyone listens to news broadcasts five or six times every day. All pleasurable things, all travel and sports and entertainment and good food and fine clothes, are in the very shortest supply, always were and always will be. There are just tiny fragments of pleasure and luxury in the world, and there is something unpatriotic about enjoying them. All foreign lands are inaccessible except to servicemen; they are vague, distant, and sealed off as though behind a curtain of plastic. The prevailing color of life in America is a dull, dark green called olive drab. That color is always respectable and always important. Most other colors risk being unpatriotic.

It is this special America, a very untypical one I guess, an unfamiliar transitional blur in the memories of most people, which is the real America for me. In that short-lived and special country we spent this summer at Devon when Finny achieved certain feats as an athlete. In such a period no one notices or rewards any achievements involving the body unless the result is to kill it or save it on the battlefield, so that there were only a few of us to applaud and wonder at what he was able to do.

One day he broke the school swimming record. He and I were fooling around in the pool, near a big bronze plaque marked with events for which the school kept records—50 yards, 100 yards, 220 yards. Under each was a slot with a marker fitted into it, showing the name of the record-holder, his year, and his time. Under "100 Yards Free Style" there was "A. Hopkins Parker—1940—53.0 seconds."

"A. Hopkins Parker?" Finny squinted up at the name. "I don't remember any A. Hopkins Parker."

"He graduated before we got here."

"You mean that record has been up there the *whole time* we've been at Devon and nobody's busted it yet?" It was an insult to the class, and Finny had tremendous loyalty to the class, as he did to any group he belonged to, beginning with him and me and radiating outward past the limits of humanity toward spirits and clouds and stars.

No one else happened to be in the pool. Around us gleamed white tile and glass brick; the green, artificial-looking water rocked gently in it shining basin, releasing vague chemical smells and a sense of many pipes and filters; even Finny's voice, trapped in this closed, high-ceilinged room, lost its special resonance and blurred into a general well of noise gathered up toward the ceiling. He said blurringly, "I have a feeling *I* can swim faster than A. Hopkins Parker."

We found a stop watch in the office. He mounted a starting box, leaned forward from the waist as he had seen racing swimmers do but never had occasion to do himself—I noticed a preparatory looseness coming into his shoulders and arms, a controlled ease about his stance which was unexpected in anyone trying to break a record. I said, "On your mark—Go!" There was a complex moment when his body uncoiled and shot forward with sudden metallic tension. He planed up the pool, his shoulders dominating the water while his legs and feet rode so low that I couldn't distinguish them; a wake rippled hurriedly by him and then at the end of the pool his position broke, he relaxed, dived, an instant's confusion and then his suddenly and metallically tense body shot back toward the other end of the pool. Another turn and up the pool again—I noticed no particular slackening of his pace—another turn, down the pool again, his hand touched the end, and he looked up at me with a composed, interested expression. "Well, how did I do?" I looked at the watch; he had broken A. Hopkins Parker's record by .7 second.

"My God! So I really did it. You know what? I thought I was going to do it. It felt as though I had that stop watch in my head and I could hear myself going just a little bit faster than A. Hopkins Parker."

"The worst thing is there weren't any witnesses. And I'm no official timekeeper. I don't think it will count."

"Well of course it won't *count*."

"You can try it again and break it again. Tomorrow. We'll get the coach in here, and all the official timekeepers and I'll call up *The Devonian* to send a reporter and a photographer—"

He climbed out of the pool. "I'm not going to do it again," he said quietly.

"Of course you are!"

"No, I just wanted to see if I could do it. Now I know. But I don't want to do it in public." Some other swimmers drifted in through the door. Finny glanced sharply at them. "By the way," he said in an even more subdued voice, "we aren't going to talk about this. It's just between you and me. Don't say anything about it, to . . . anyone."

"Not say anything about it! When you broke the school record!"

"*Sh-h-h-h-h!*" He shot a blazing, agitated glance at me.

I stopped and looked at him up and down. He didn't look directly back at me. "You're too good to be true," I said after a while.

He glanced at me, and then said, "Thanks a lot" in a somewhat expressionless voice.

Was he trying to impress me or something? Not tell anybody? When he had broken a school record without a day of practice? I knew he was serious about it, so I didn't tell anybody. Perhaps for that reason his accomplishment took root in my mind and grew rapidly in the darkness where I was forced to hide it. The Devon School record books contained a mistake, a lie, and nobody knew it but Finny and me. A. Hopkins Parker was living in a fool's paradise, wherever he was. His defeated name remained in bronze on the school record plaque, while Finny deliberately evaded an athletic honor. It was true that he had many already—the Winslow Galbraith Memorial Football Trophy for having brought the most Christian sportsmanship to the game during the 1941–1942 season, the Margaret Duke Bonaventura ribbon and prize for the student who conducted himself at hockey most like the way her son had done, the Devon School Contact Sport Award, Presented Each Year to That Student Who in the Opinion of the Athletic Advisors Excels His Fellows in the Sportsmanlike Performance of Any Game Involving Bodily Contact. But these were in the past, and they were prizes, not school records. The sports Finny played officially—football, hockey, baseball, lacrosse—didn't have school records. To switch to a new sport suddenly, just for a day, and immediately break a record in it—that was about as neat a trick, as dazzling a reversal as I could, to be perfectly honest, possibly imagine. There was something inebriating in the suppleness of this feat. When I thought about it my head felt a little dizzy and my stomach began to tingle. It had, in one word, glamour, absolute schoolboy glamour. When I looked down at that stop watch and realized a split second before I permitted my face to show it or my voice to announce it that Finny had broken a school record, I had experienced a feeling that also can be described in one word—shock.

To keep silent about this amazing happening deepened the shock for me. It made Finny seem too unusual for—not friendship, but too unusual for rivalry. And there were few relationships among us at Devon not based on rivalry.

"Swimming in pools is screwy anyway," he said after a long, unusual silence as we walked toward the dormitory. "The only real swimming is in the ocean." Then in the everyday, mediocre tone he used when he was proposing something really outrageous, he added, "Let's go to the beach."

The beach was hours away by bicycle, forbidden, completely out of all bounds. Going there risked expulsion, destroyed the studying I was going to do for an important test the next morning, blasted the reasonable amount of order I wanted to maintain in my life, and it also involved the kind of long, labored bicycle ride I hated. "All right," I said.

We got our bikes and slipped away from Devon along a back road. Having invited me Finny now felt he had to keep me entertained. He told long, wild stories about his childhood; as I pumped panting up steep hills he glided along beside me, joking steadily. He analyzed my character, and he insisted on knowing what I disliked most about him ("You're too conventional," I said). He rode backward with no hands, he rode on his own handlebars, he jumped off and back on his moving bike as he had seen trick horseback riders do in the movies. He sang. Despite the steady musical undertone in his speaking voice Finny couldn't carry a tune, and he couldn't remember the melody or the words to any song. But he loved listening to music, any music, and he liked to sing.

We reached the beach late in the afternoon. The tide was high and the surf was heavy. I dived in and rode a couple of waves, but they had reached that stage of power in which you could feel the whole strength of the ocean in them. The second wave, as it tore toward the beach with me, spewed me a little ahead of it, encroaching rapidly; suddenly it was immeasurably bigger than I was, it rushed me from the control of gravity and took control of me itself; the wave threw me down in a primitive plunge without a bottom, then there was a bottom, grinding sand, and I skidded onto the shore. The wave hesitated, balanced there, and then hissed back toward the deep water, its tentacles not quite interested enough in me to drag me with it.

I made my way up on the beach and lay down. Finny came, ceremoniously took my pulse, and then went back into the ocean. He stayed in an hour, breaking off every few minutes to come back to me and talk. The sand was so hot from the all-day sunshine that I had to brush the top layer away in order to lie down on it, and Finny's progress across the beach became a series of high, startled leaps.

The ocean, throwing up foaming sun-sprays across some nearby rocks, was winter cold. This kind of sunshine and ocean, with the accumulating roar of the surf and the salty, adventurous, flirting wind from the sea, always intoxicated Phineas. He was everywhere, he enjoyed himself hugely, he laughed out loud at passing sea gulls. And he did everything he could think of for me.

We had dinner at a hot dog stand, with our backs to the ocean and its now cooler wind, our faces toward the heat of the cooking range. Then we walked on toward the center of the beach, where there was a subdued New England strip of honky-tonks. The Boardwalk lights against the deepening blue sky gained an ideal, starry beauty and the lights from the belt of honky-tonks and shooting galleries and beer gardens gleamed with a quiet purity in the clear twilight.

Finny and I went along the Boardwalk in our sneakers and white slacks, Finny in a light blue polo shirt and I in a T-shirt. I noticed that people were looking fixedly at him, so I took a look myself to see why. His skin radiated a reddish copper glow of tan, his brown hair had been a little bleached by the sun, and I noticed that the tan made his eyes shine with a cool blue-green fire.

"Everybody's staring at you," he suddenly said to me. "It's because of that movie-star tan you picked up this afternoon . . . showing off again."

Enough broken rules were enough that night. Neither of us suggested going into any of the honky-tonks or beer gardens. We did have one glass of beer each at a fairly respectable-looking bar, convincing, or seeming to convince the bartender that we were old enough by a show of forged draft cards. Then we found a good spot among some sand dunes at the lonely end of the beach, and there we settled down to sleep for the night. The last words of Finny's usual nighttime monologue were, "I hope you're having a pretty good time here. I know I kind of dragged you away at the point of a gun, but after all you can't come to the shore with just anybody and you can't come by yourself, and at this teen-age period in life the proper person is your best pal." He hesitated and then added, "which is what you are," and there was silence on his dune.

It was a courageous thing to say. Exposing a sincere emotion nakedly like that at the Devon School was the next thing to suicide. I should have told him then that he was my best friend also and rounded off what he had said. I started to; I nearly did. But something held me back. Perhaps I was stopped by that level of feeling, deeper than thought, which contains the truth.

4

The next morning I saw dawn for the first time. It began not as the gorgeous fanfare over the ocean I had expected, but as a strange gray thing, like sunshine seen through burlap. I looked over to see if Phineas was awake. He was still asleep, although in this drained light he looked more dead than asleep. The ocean looked dead too, dead gray waves hissing mordantly along the beach, which was gray and dead-looking itself.

I turned over and tried to sleep again but couldn't, and so lay on my back looking at this gray burlap sky. Very gradually, like one instrument after another being tentatively rehearsed, beacons of color began to pierce the sky. The ocean perked up a little from the reflection of these colored slivers in the sky. Bright high lights shone on the tips of waves, and beneath its gray surface I could see lurking a deep midnight green. The beach shed its deadness and became a spectral gray-white, then more white than gray, and finally it was totally white and stainless, as pure as the shores of Eden. Phineas, still asleep on his dune, made me think of Lazarus, brought back to life by the touch of God.

I didn't contemplate this transformation for long.

Inside my head, for as long as I could remember, there had always been a sense of time ticking steadily. I looked at the sky and the ocean and knew that it was around six-thirty. The ride back to Devon would take three hours at least. My important test, trigonometry, was going to be held at ten o'clock.

Phineas woke up talking. "That was one of the best night's sleep I ever had."

"When did you ever have a bad one?"

"The time I broke my ankle in football. I like the way this beach looks now. Shall we have a morning swim?"

"Are you crazy? It's too late for that."

"What time is it anyway?" Finny knew I was a walking clock.

"It's going on seven o'clock."

"There's time for just a short swim," and before I could say anything he was trotting down the beach, shedding clothes as he went, and into the ocean. I waited for him where I was. He came back after a while full of chilly glow and energy and talk. I didn't have much to say. "Do you have the money?" I asked once, suddenly suspecting that he had lost our joint seventy-five cents during the night. There was a search, a hopeless one, in the sand, and so we set off on the long ride back without any breakfast, and got to Devon just in time for my test. I flunked it; I knew I was going to as soon as I looked at the test problems. It was the first test I had ever flunked.

But Finny gave me little time to worry about that. Right after lunch there was a game of blitzball which took most of the afternoon, and right after dinner there was the meeting of the Super Suicide Society of the Summer Session.

That night in our room, even though I was worn out

from all the exercise, I tried to catch up to what had been happening in trigonometry.

"You work too hard," Finny said, sitting opposite me at the table where we read. The study lamp cast a round yellow pool between us. "You know all about History and English and French and everything else. What good will Trigonometry do you?"

"I'll have to pass it to graduate, for one thing."

"Don't give me that line. Nobody at Devon has ever been surer of graduating than you are. You aren't working for *that*. You want to be head of the class, valedictorian, so you can make a speech on Graduation Day—in Latin or something boring like that probably—and be the boy wonder of the school. I know you."

"Don't be stupid. I wouldn't waste my time on anything like that."

"You never waste your time. That's why I have to do it for you."

"Anyway," I grudgingly added, "somebody's got to be the head of the class."

"You see, I knew that's what you were aiming at," he concluded quietly.

"Fooey."

What if I was. It was a pretty good goal to have, it seemed to me. After all, he should talk. He had won and been proud to win the Galbraith Football Trophy and the Contact Sport Award, and there were two or three other athletic prizes he was sure to get this year or next. If I was head of the class on Graduation Day and made a speech and won the Ne Plus Ultra Scholastic Achievement Citation, then we would both have come out on top, we would be even, that was all. We would be even. . . .

Was that it! My eyes snapped from the textbook

toward him. Did he notice this sudden glance shot
across the pool of light? He didn't seem to; he went
on writing down his strange curlicue notes about
Thomas Hardy in Phineas Shorthand. *Was that it!*
With his head bent over in the lamplight I could discern a slight mound in his brow above the eyebrows,
the faint bulge which is usually believed to indicate
mental power. Phineas would be the first to disclaim
any great mental power in himself. But what did go
on in his mind? If I was the head of the class and won
that prize, then we would be even. . . .

His head started to come up, and mine snapped
down. I glared at the textbook. "Relax," he said.
"Your brain'll explode if you keep this up."

"You don't need to worry about me, Finny."

"I'm not worried."

"You wouldn't—" I wasn't sure I had the control to
put this question—"mind if I wound up head of the
class, would you?"

"Mind?" Two clear green-blue eyes looked at me.
"Fat chance you've got, anyway, with Chet Douglass
around."

"But you wouldn't mind, would you?" I repeated in
a lower and more distinct voice.

He gave me that half-smile of his, which had won
him a thousand conflicts. "I'd kill myself out of jealous
envy."

I believed him. The joking manner was a screen; I
believed him. In front of my eyes the trigonometry
textbook blurred into a jumble. I couldn't see. My
brain exploded. He minded, despised the possibility
that I might be the head of the school. There was a
swift chain of explosions in my brain, one certainty
after another blasted—up like a detonation went the
idea of any best friend, up went affection and partner-

ship and sticking by someone and relying on someone absolutely in the jungle of a boys' school, up went the hope that there was anyone in this school—in this world—whom I could trust. "Chet Douglass," I said uncertainly, "is a sure thing for it."

My misery was too deep to speak any more. I scanned the page; I was having trouble breathing, as though the oxygen were leaving the room. Amid its devastation my mind flashed from thought to thought, despairingly in search of something left which it could rely on. Not rely on absolutely, that was obliterated as a possibility, just rely on a little, some solace, something surviving in the ruins.

I found it. I found a single sustaining thought. The thought was, You and Phineas are even already. You are even in enmity. You are both coldly driving ahead for yourselves alone. You did hate him for breaking that school swimming record, but so what? He hated you for getting an A in every course but one last term. You would have had an A in that one except for him. Except for him.

Then a second realization broke as clearly and bleakly as dawn at the beach. Finny had deliberately set out to wreck my studies. That explained blitzball, that explained the nightly meetings of the Super Suicide Society, that explained his insistence that I share all his diversions. The way I believed that you're-my-best-friend blabber! The shadow falling across his face if I didn't want to do something with him! His instinct for sharing everything with me? Sure, he wanted to share everything with me, especially his procession of D's in every subject. That way he, the great athlete, would be way ahead of me. It was all cold trickery, it was all calculated, it was all enmity.

I felt better. Yes, I sensed it like the sweat of relief

when nausea passes away; I felt better. We were even
after all, even in enmity. The deadly rivalry was on
both sides after all.

I became quite a student after that. I had always
been a good one, although I wasn't really interested
and excited by learning itself, the way Chet Douglass
was. Now I became not just good but exceptional,
with Chet Douglass my only rival in sight. But I began
to see that Chet was weakened by the very genuine-
ness of his interest in learning. He got carried away by
things; for example, he was so fascinated by the tilting
planes of solid geometry that he did almost as badly
in trigonometry as I did myself. When we read *Can-
dide* it opened up a new way of looking at the world
to Chet, and he continued hungrily reading Voltaire,
in French, while the class went on to other people. He
was vulnerable there, because to me they were all
pretty much alike—Voltaire and Molière and the laws
of motion and the Magna Carta and the Pathetic Fal-
lacy and *Tess of the D'Urbervilles*—and I worked indiscriminately on all of them.

Finny had no way of knowing this, because it all
happened so far ahead of him scholastically. In class
he generally sat slouched in his chair, his alert face
following the discussion with an expression of philo-
sophical comprehension, and when he was forced to
speak himself the hypnotic power of his voice combined with the singularity of his mind to produce an-
swers which were often not right but could rarely be
branded as wrong. Written tests were his downfall
because he could not speak them, and as a result he
got grades which were barely passing. It wasn't that
he never worked, because he did work, in short, intense bouts now and then. As that crucial summer

wore on and I tightened the discipline on myself Phineas increased his bouts of studying.

I could see through that. I was more and more certainly becoming the best student in the school; Phineas was without question the best athlete, so in that way we were even. But while he was a very poor student I was a pretty good athlete, and when everything was thrown into the scales they would in the end tilt definitely toward me. The new attacks of studying were his emergency measures to save himself. I redoubled my effort.

It was surprising how well we got along in these weeks. Sometimes I found it hard to remember his treachery, sometimes I discovered myself thoughtlessly slipping back into affection for him again. It was hard to remember when one summer day after another broke with a cool effulgence over us, and there was a breath of widening life in the morning air —something hard to describe—an oxygen intoxicant, a shining northern paganism, some odor, some feeling so hopelessly promising that I would fall back in my bed on guard against it. It was hard to remember in the heady and sensual clarity of these mornings; I forgot whom I hated and who hated me. I wanted to break out crying from stabs of hopeless joy, or intolerable promise, or because these mornings were too full of beauty for me, because I knew of too much hate to be contained in a world like this.

Summer lazed on. No one paid any attention to us. One day I found myself describing to Mr. Prud'homme how Phineas and I had slept on the beach, and he seemed to be quite interested in it, in all the details, so much so that he missed the point: that we had flatly broken a basic rule.

No one cared, no one exercised any real discipline over us; we were on our own.

August arrived with a deepening of all the summer-time splendors of New Hampshire. Early in the month we had two days of light, steady rain which aroused a final fullness everywhere. The branches of the old trees, which had been familiar to me either half-de-nuded or completely gaunt during the winter terms at Devon, now seemed about to break from their storms of leaves. Little disregarded patches of ground revealed that they had been gardens all along, and nondescript underbrush around the gymnasium and the river broke into color. There was a latent freshness in the air, as though spring were returning in the middle of the summer.

But examinations were at hand. I wasn't as ready for them as I wanted to be. The Suicide Society continued to meet every evening, and I continued to attend, because I didn't want Finny to understand me as I understood him.

And also I didn't want to let him excel me in this, even though I knew that it didn't matter whether he showed me up at the tree or not. Because it was what you had in your heart that counted. And I had detected that Finny's was a den of lonely, selfish ambition. He was no better than I was, no matter who won all the contests.

A French examination was announced for one Friday late in August. Finny and I studied for it in the library Thursday afternoon; I went over vocabulary lists, and he wrote messages—je ne give a damn pas about le francais, les filles en France ne wear pas les pantelons—and passed them with great seriousness to me, as *aide-mémoire*. Of course I didn't get any work done. After supper I went to our room to try again. Phineas came in a couple of minutes later.

"Arise," he began airily, "Senior Overseer Charter Member! Elwin 'Leper' Lepellier has announced his intention to make the leap this very night, to qualify, to save his face at last."

I didn't believe it for a second. Leper Lepellier would go down paralyzed with panic on any sinking troopship before making such a jump. Finny had put him up to it, to finish me for good on the exam. I turned around with elaborate resignation. "If he jumps out of that tree I'm Mahatma Gandhi."

"All right," agreed Finny absently. He had a way of turning clichés inside out like that. "Come on, let's go. We've got to be there. You never know, maybe he *will* do it this time."

"Oh, for God sake." I slammed closed the French book.

"What's the matter?"

What a performance! His face was completely questioning and candid.

"Studying!" I snarled. "Studying! You know, books. Work. Examinations."

"Yeah . . ." He waited for me to go on, as though he didn't see what I was getting at.

"Oh for God sake! You don't know what I'm talking about. No, of course not. Not you." I stood up and slammed the chair against the desk. "Okay, we go. We watch little lily-liver Lepellier not jump from the tree, and I ruin my grade."

He looked at me with an interested, surprised expression. "You want to study?"

I began to feel a little uneasy at this mildness of his, so I sighed heavily. "Never mind, forget it. I know, I joined the club, I'm going. What else can I do?"

"Don't go." He said it very simply and casually, as though he were saying, "Nice day." He shrugged, "Don't go. What the hell, it's only a game."

I had stopped halfway across the room, and now I just looked at him. "What d'you mean?" I muttered. What he meant was clear enough, but I was groping for what lay behind his words, for what his thoughts could possibly be. I might have asked, "Who are you, then?" instead. I was facing a total stranger.

"I didn't know you needed to *study*," he said simply, "I didn't think you ever did. I thought it just came to you."

It seemed that he had made some kind of parallel between my studies and his sports. He probably thought anything you were good at came without effort. He didn't know yet that he was unique.

I couldn't quite achieve a normal speaking voice. "If I need to study, then so do you."

"Me?" He smiled faintly. "Listen, I could study forever and I'd never break C. But it's different for you, you're good. You really are. If I had a brain like that, I'd—I'd have my head cut open so people could look at it."

"Now wait a second . . ."

He put his hands on the back of a chair and leaned toward me. "I know. We kid around a lot and everything, but you have to be serious sometime, about something. If you're really good at something, I mean if there's nobody, or hardly anybody, who's as good as you are, then you've got to be serious about that. Don't mess around, for God's sake." He frowned disapprovingly at me. "Why didn't you say you had to study before? Don't move from that desk. It's going to be all A's for you."

"Wait a minute," I said, without any reason.

"It's okay. I'll oversee old Leper. I know he's not going to do it." He was at the door.

"Wait a minute," I said more sharply. "Wait just a minute. I'm coming."

"No you aren't, pal, you're going to study."

"Never mind my studying."

"You think you've done enough already?"

"Yes." I let this drop curtly to bar him from telling me what to do about my work. He let it go at that, and went out the door ahead of me, whistling off key.

We followed our gigantic shadows across the campus, and Phineas began talking in wild French, to give me a little extra practice. I said nothing, my mind exploring the new dimensions of isolation around me. Any fear I had ever had of the tree was nothing beside this. It wasn't my neck, but my understanding which was menaced. He had never been jealous of me for a second. Now I knew that there never was and never could have been any rivalry between us. I was not of the same quality as he.

I couldn't stand this. We reached the others loitering around the base of the tree, and Phineas began exuberantly to throw off his clothes, delighted by the fading glow of the day, the challenge of the tree, the competitive tension of all of us. He lived and flourished in such moments. "Let's go, you and me," he called. A new idea struck him. "We'll go together, a double jump! Neat, eh?"

None of this mattered now; I would have listlessly agreed to anything. He started up the wooden rungs and I began climbing behind, up to the limb high over the bank. Phineas ventured a little way along it, holding a thin nearby branch for support. "Come out a little way," he said, "and then we'll jump side by side." The countryside was striking from here, a deep green sweep of playing fields and bordering shrubbery, with the school stadium white and miniature-looking across the river. From behind us the last long rays of light played across the campus, accenting every slight undulation of the land, emphasizing the separateness of each bush.

Holding firmly to the trunk, I took a step toward him, and then my knees bent and I jounced the limb. Finny, his balance gone, swung his head around to look at me for an instant with extreme interest, and then he tumbled sideways, broke through the little branches below and hit the bank with a sickening, unnatural thud. It was the first clumsy physical action I had ever seen him make. With unthinking sureness I moved out on the limb and jumped into the river, every trace of my fear of this forgotten.

5

None of us was allowed near the infirmary during the next days, but I heard all the rumors that came out of it. Eventually a fact emerged; it was one of his legs, which had been "shattered." I couldn't figure out exactly what this word meant, whether it meant broken in one or several places, cleanly or badly, and I didn't ask. I learned no more, although the subject was discussed endlessly. Out of my hearing people must have talked of other things, but everyone talked about Phineas to me. I suppose this was only natural. I had been right beside him when it happened, I was his roommate.

The effect of his injury on the masters seemed deeper than after other disasters I remembered there. It was as though they felt it was especially unfair that it should strike one of the sixteen-year-olds, one of the few young men who could be free and happy in the summer of 1942.

I couldn't go on hearing about it much longer. If anyone had been suspicious of me, I might have developed some strength to defend myself. But there was nothing. No one suspected. Phineas must still be too sick, or too noble, to tell them.

I spent as much time as I could alone in our room,

trying to empty my mind of every thought, to forget where I was, even who I was. One evening when I was dressing for dinner in this numbed frame of mind, an idea occurred to me, the first with any energy behind it since Finny fell from the tree. I decided to put on his clothes. We wore the same size, and although he always criticized mine he used to wear them frequently, quickly forgetting what belonged to him and what to me. I never forgot, and that evening I put on his cordovan shoes, his pants, and I looked for and finally found his pink shirt, neatly laundered in a drawer. Its high, somewhat stiff collar against my neck, the wide cuffs touching my wrists, the rich material against my skin excited a sense of strangeness and distinction; I felt like some nobleman, some Spanish grandee.

But when I looked in the mirror it was no remote aristocrat I had become, no character out of daydreams. I was Phineas, Phineas to the life. I even had his humorous expression in my face, his sharp, optimistic awareness. I had no idea why this gave me such intense relief, but it seemed, standing there in Finny's triumphant shirt, that I would never stumble through the confusions of my own character again.

I didn't go down to dinner. The sense of transformation stayed with me throughout the evening, and even when I undressed and went to bed. That night I slept easily, and it was only on waking up that this illusion was gone, and I was confronted with myself, and what I had done to Finny.

Sooner or later it had to happen, and that morning it did. "Finny's better!" Dr. Stanpole called to me on the chapel steps over the organ recessional thundering behind us. I made my way haltingly past the members of the choir with their black robes flapping in the morning breeze, the doctor's words reverberating around me. He might denounce me there before the whole school. Instead he steered me amiably into the lane leading toward the infirmary. "He could stand a visitor or two now, after these very nasty few days."

"You don't think I'll upset him or anything?"

"You? No, why? I don't want any of these teachers flapping around him. But a pal or two, it'll do him good."

"I suppose he's still pretty sick."

"It was a messy break."

"But how does he—how is he feeling? I mean, is he cheerful at all, or—"

"Oh, you know Finny." I didn't, I was pretty sure I didn't know Finny at all. "It was a messy break," he went on, "but we'll have him out of it eventually. He'll be walking again."

"*Walking* again!"

"Yes." The doctor didn't look at me, and barely changed his tone of voice. "Sports are finished for him, after an accident like that. Of course."

"But he must be able to," I burst out, "if his leg's still there, if you aren't going to amputate it—you aren't, are you?—then if it isn't amputated and the bones are still there, then it must come back the way it was, why wouldn't it? Of course it will."

Dr. Stanpole hesitated, and I think glanced at me for a moment. "Sports are finished. As a friend you ought to help him face that and accept it. The sooner he does the better off he'll be. If I had the slightest hope that he could do more than walk I'd be all for trying for everything. There is no such hope. I'm sorry, as of course everyone is. It's a tragedy, but there it is."

I grabbed my head, fingers digging into my skin, and the doctor, thinking to be kind, put his hand on my shoulder. At his touch I lost all hope of controlling myself. I burst out crying into my hands; I cried for Phineas and for myself and for this doctor who believed in facing things. Most of all I cried because of kindness, which I had not expected.

"Now that's no good. You've got to be cheerful and hopeful. He needs that from you. He wanted especially to see you. You were the one person he asked for."

That stopped my tears. I brought my hands down and watched the red brick exterior of the infirmary, a cheerful building, coming closer. Of course I was the first person he wanted to see. Phineas would say nothing behind my back; he would accuse me, face to face.

We were walking up the steps of the infirmary, everything was very swift, and next I was in a corridor being nudged by Dr. Stanpole toward a door. "He's in there. I'll be with you in a minute."

The door was slightly ajar, and I pushed it back and stood transfixed on the threshold. Phineas lay among pillows and sheets, his left leg, enormous in its white bindings, suspended a little above the bed. A tube led from a glass bottle into his right arm. Some channel began to close inside me and I knew I was about to black out.

"Come on in," I heard him say. "You look worse than I do." The fact that he could still make a light remark pulled me back a little, and I went to a chair beside his bed. He seemed to have diminished physically in the few days which had passed, and to have lost his tan. His eyes studied me as though I were the patient. They no longer had their sharp good humor, but had become clouded and visionary. After a while I realized he had been given a drug. "What are *you* looking so sick about?" he went on.

"Finny, I—" there was no controlling what I said, the words were instinctive, like the reactions of someone cornered. "What happened there at the tree? That goddam tree, I'm going to cut down that tree. Who cares who can jump out of it. What happened, what happened? How did you fall, how could you fall off like that?"

"I just fell," his eyes were vaguely on my face, "something jiggled and I fell over. I remember I turned around and looked at you, it was like I had all the time in the world. I thought I could reach out and get hold of you."

I flinched violently away from him. "To drag me down too!"

He kept looking vaguely over my face. "To get hold of you, so I wouldn't fall off."

"Yes, naturally." I was fighting for air in this close room. "I tried, you remember? I reached out but you were gone, you went down through those little branches underneath, and when I reached out there was only air."

"I just remember looking at your face for a second. Awfully funny expression you had. Very shocked, like you have right now."

"Right now? Well, of course, I *am* shocked. Who wouldn't be shocked, for God sakes. It's terrible, everything's terrible."

"But I don't see why you should look so *personally* shocked. You look like it happened to you or something."

"It's almost like it did! I was right there, right on the limb beside you."

"Yes, I know. I remember it all."

There was a hard block of silence, and then I said

quietly, as though my words might detonate the room, "Do you remember what made you fall?"

His eyes continued their roaming across my face. "I don't know, I must have just lost my balance. It must have been that. I did have this idea, this feeling that when you were standing there beside me, y— I don't know, I had a kind of feeling. But you can't say anything for sure from just feelings. And this feeling doesn't make any sense. It was a crazy idea, I must have been delirious. So I just have to forget it. I just fell," he turned away to grope for something among the pillows, "that's all." Then he glanced back at me, "I'm sorry about that feeling I had."

I couldn't say anything to this sincere, drugged apology for having suspected the truth. He was never going to accuse me. It was only a feeling he had, and at this moment he must have been formulating a new commandment in his personal decalogue: ⌈Never accuse a friend of a crime if you only have a feeling he did it. ⌉

And I thought we were competitors! It was so ludicrous I wanted to cry.

If Phineas had been sitting here in this pool of guilt, how would he have felt, what would he have done?

He would have told me the truth.

I got up so suddenly that the chair overturned. I stared at him in amazement, and he stared back, his mouth breaking into a grin as the moments passed. "Well," he said at last in his friendly, knowing voice, "what are you going to do, hypnotize me?"

"Finny, I've got something to tell you. You're going to hate it, but there's something I've got to tell you."

"My God, what energy," he said, falling back against the pillows. "You sound like General MacArthur."

"I don't care who I sound like, and you won't think so when I tell you. This is the worst thing in the world, and I'm sorry and I hate to tell you but I've got to tell you."

But I didn't tell him. Dr. Stanpole came in before I was able to, and then a nurse came in, and I was sent away. The next day the doctor decided that Finny was not yet well enough to see visitors, even old pals like me. Soon after he was taken in an ambulance to his home outside Boston.

The Summer Session closed, officially came to an end. But to me it seemed irresolutely suspended, halted strangely before its time. I went south for a month's vacation in my home town and spent it in an atmosphere of reverie and unreality, as though I had lived that month once already and had not been interested by it the first time either.

At the end of September I started back toward Devon on the jammed, erratic trains of September, 1942. I reached Boston seventeen hours behind schedule; there would be prestige in that at Devon, where those of us from long distances with travel adventures to report or invent held the floor for several days after a vacation.

By luck I got a taxi at South Station, and instead of saying "North Station" to the driver, instead of just crossing Boston and catching the final train for the short last leg of the trip to Devon, instead of that I sat back in the seat and heard myself give the address of Finny's house on the outskirts.

We found it fairly easily, on a street with a nave of ancient elms branching over it. The house itself was high, white, and oddly proper to be the home of Phineas. It presented a face of definite elegance to the street, although behind that wings and ells dwindled quickly in formality until the house ended in a big plain barn.

Nothing surprised Phineas. A cleaning woman answered the door and when I came into the room where he was sitting, he looked very pleased and not at all surprised.

"So you *are* going to show up!" his voice took off in one of its flights, "and you brought me something to eat from down South, didn't you? Honeysuckle and molasses or something like that?" I tried to think of something funny. "Corn bread? You did bring something. You didn't go all the way to Dixie and then come back with nothing but your dismal face to show for it." His talk rolled on, ignoring and covering my look of shock and clumsiness. I was silenced by the sight of him propped by white hospital-looking pillows in a big armchair. Despite everything at the Devon Infirmary, he had seemed an athlete there, temporarily injured in a game; as though the trainer would come in any minute and tape him up. Propped now before a great New England fireplace, on this quiet old street, he looked to me like an invalid, house-bound.

"I brought . . . Well I never remember to bring anyone anything." I struggled to get my voice above this self-accusing murmur. "I'll send you something. Flowers or something."

"Flowers! What happened to you in Dixie anyway?"

"Well then," there was no light remark anywhere in my head, "I'll get you some books."

"Never mind about books. I'd rather have some talk. What happened down South?"

"As a matter of fact," I brought out all the cheerfulness I could find for this, "there was a fire. It was just a grass fire out behind our house. We . . . took some brooms and beat it. I guess what we really did was fan it because it just kept getting bigger until the Fire Department finally came. They could tell where it was because of all the flaming brooms we were waving around in the air, trying to put them out."

Finny liked that story. But it put us on the familiar friendly level, pals trading stories. How was I going to begin talking about it? It would not be just a thunderbolt. It wouldn't even seem real.

Not in this conversation, not in this room. I wished I had met him in a railroad station, or at some highway intersection. Not here. Here the small window panes shone from much polishing and the walls were hung with miniatures and old portraits. The chairs were either heavily upholstered and too comfortable to stay awake in or Early American and never used. There were several square, solid tables covered with family pictures and random books and magazines, and also three small, elegant tables not used for anything. It was a compromise of a room, with a few good "pieces" for guests to look at, and the rest of it for people to use.

But I had known Finny in an impersonal dormitory, a gym, a playing field. In the room we shared at Devon many strangers had lived before us, and many would afterward. It was there that I had done it, but it was here that I would have to tell it. I felt like a wild man who had stumbled in from the jungle to tear the place apart.

I moved back in the Early American chair. Its rigid back and high armrests immediately forced me into a righteous posture. My blood could start to pound if it wanted to; let it. I was going ahead. "I was thinking about you most of the trip up."

"Oh yeah?" He glanced briefly into my eyes.

"I was thinking about you . . . and the accident."

"There's loyalty for you. To think about me when you were on a vacation."

"I was thinking about it . . . about you because—I was thinking about you and the accident because I caused it."

Finny looked steadily at me, his face very handsome and expressionless. "What do you mean, you caused it?" his voice was as steady as his eyes.

My own voice sounded quiet and foreign. "I jounced the limb. I caused it." One more sentence. "I deliberately jounced the limb so you would fall off."

He looked older than I had ever seen him. "Of course you didn't."

"Yes I did. I did!"

"Of course you didn't do it. You damn fool. Sit down, you damn fool."

"Of course I did!"

"I'm going to hit you if you don't sit down."

"*Hit* me!" I looked at him. "*Hit* me! You can't even get up! You can't even come near me!"

"I'll kill you if you don't shut up."

"You see! Kill me! Now you know what it is! I did it because I felt like that! Now you know yourself!"

"I don't know anything. Go away. I'm tired and you make me sick. Go away." He held his forehead wearily, an unlikely way.

It struck me then that I was injuring him again. It occurred to me that this could be an even deeper injury than what I had done before. I would have to back out of it, I would have to disown it. Could it be that he might even be right? Had I really and definitely and knowingly done it to him after all? I couldn't remember, I couldn't think. However it was, it was worse for him to know it. I had to take it back.

But not here. "You'll be back at Devon in a few

weeks, won't you?" I muttered after both of us had sat in silence for a while.

"Sure, I'll be there by Thanksgiving anyway."

At Devon, where every stick of furniture didn't assert that Finny was a part of it, I could make it up to him.

Now I had to get out of there. There was only one way to do it; I would have to make every move false. "I've had an awfully long trip," I said, "I never sleep much on trains. I guess I'm not making too much sense today."

"Don't worry about it."

"I think I'd better get to the station. I'm already a day late at Devon."

"You aren't going to start living by the rules, are you?"

I grinned at him. "Oh no, I wouldn't do that," and that was the most false thing, the biggest lie of all.

6

Peace had deserted Devon. Although not in the look of the campus and village; they retained much of their dreaming summer calm. Fall had barely touched the full splendor of the trees, and during the height of the day the sun briefly regained its summertime power. In the air there was only an edge of coolness to imply the coming winter.

But all had been caught up, like the first fallen leaves, by a new and energetic wind. The Summer Session—a few dozen boys being force-fed education, a stopgap while most of the masters were away and most of the traditions stored against sultriness—the Summer Session was over. It had been the school's first, but this was its one hundred and sixty-third Winter Session, and the forces reassembled for it scattered the easygoing summer spirit like so many fallen leaves.

The masters were in their places for the first Chapel, seated in stalls in front of and at right angles to us, suggesting by their worn expressions and careless postures that they had never been away at all.

In an apse of the church sat their wives and children, the objects during the tedious winter months of our ceaseless, ritual speculation (Why did he ever marry *her*? What in the world ever made her marry

64

him? How could the two of them ever have produced *those* little monsters?). The masters favored seersucker on this mild first day, the wives broke out their hats. Five of the younger teachers were missing, gone into the war. Mr. Pike had come in his Naval ensign's uniform; some reflex must have survived Midshipman's School and brought him back to Devon for the day. His face was as mild and hopeless as ever; mooning above the snappy, rigid blouse, it gave him the air of an impostor.

Continuity was the keynote. The same hymns were played, the same sermon given, the same announcements made. There was one surprise; maids had disappeared "for the Duration," a new phase then. But continuity was stressed, not beginning again but continuing the education of young men according to the unbroken traditions of Devon.

I knew, perhaps I alone knew, that this was false. Devon had slipped through their fingers during the warm overlooked months. The traditions had been broken, the standards let down, all rules forgotten. In those bright days of truancy we had never thought of What We Owed Devon, as the sermon this opening day exhorted us to do. We had thought of ourselves, of what Devon owed us, and we had taken all of that and much more. Today's hymn was *Dear Lord and Father of Mankind Forgive Our Foolish Ways;* we had never heard that during the summer either. Ours had been a wayward gypsy music, leading us down all kinds of foolish gypsy ways, unforgiven. I was glad of it, I had almost caught the rhythm of it, the dancing, clicking jangle of it during the summer.

Still it had come to an end, in the last long rays of daylight at the tree, when Phineas fell. It was forced on me as I sat chilled through the Chapel service, that this probably vindicated the rules of Devon after all, wintery Devon. If you broke the rules, then they broke you. That, I think, was the real point of the sermon on this first morning.

After the service ended we set out seven hundred strong, the regular winter throng of the Devon School, to hustle through our lists of appointments. All classrooms were crowded, swarms were on the crosswalks, the dormitories were as noisy as factories, every bulletin board was a forest of notices.

We had been an idiosyncratic, leaderless band in the summer, undirected except by the eccentric notions of Phineas. Now the official class leaders and politicians could be seen taking charge, assuming as a matter of course their control of these walks and fields which had belonged only to us. I had the same room which Finny and I had shared during the summer, but across the hall, in the large suite where Leper Lepellier had dreamed his way through July and August amid sunshine and dust motes and windows through which the ivy had reached tentatively into the room, here Brinker Hadley had established his headquarters. Emissaries were already dropping in to confer with him. Leper, luckless in his last year as all the others, had been moved to a room lost in an old building off somewhere in the trees toward the gym.

After morning classes and lunch I went across to see Brinker, started into the room and then stopped. Suddenly I did not want to see the trays of snails which Leper had passed the summer collecting replaced by Brinker's files. Not yet. Although it was something to have this year's dominant student across the way. Ordinarily he should have been a magnet for me, the center of all the excitement and influences in the class. Ordinarily this would have been so—if the summer, the gypsy days, had not intervened. Now Brinker, with his steady wit and ceaseless plans, Brinker had nothing to offer in place of Leper's dust motes and creeping ivy and snails.

I didn't go in. In any case I was late for my afternoon appointment. I never used to be late. But today I was, later even than I had to be. I was supposed to report to the Crew House, down on the banks of the lower river. There are two rivers at Devon, divided by a small dam. On my way I stopped on the footbridge which crosses the top of the dam separating them and looked upstream, at the narrow little Devon River sliding toward me between its thick fringe of pine and birch.

As I had to do whenever I glimpsed this river, I thought of Phineas. Not of the tree and pain, but of one of his favorite tricks, Phineas in exaltation, balancing on one foot on the prow of a canoe like a river god, his raised arms invoking the air to support him, face transfigured, body a complex set of balances and compensations, each muscle aligned in perfection with all the others to maintain this supreme fantasy of achievement, his skin glowing from immersions, his whole body hanging between river and sky as though he had transcended gravity and might by gently pushing upward with his foot glide a little way higher and remain suspended in space, encompassing all the glory of the summer and offering it to the sky.

Then, an infinitesimal veering of the canoe, and the line of his body would break, the soaring arms collapse, up shoot an uncontrollable leg, and Phineas would tumble into the water, roaring with rage.

I stopped in the middle of this hurrying day to remember him like that, and then, feeling refreshed, I went on to the Crew House beside the tidewater river below the dam.

We had never used this lower river, the Naguamsett, during the summer. It was ugly, saline, fringed with marsh, mud and seaweed. A few miles away it was joined to the ocean, so that its movements were governed by unimaginable factors like the Gulf Stream, the Polar Ice Cap, and the moon. It was nothing like the fresh-water Devon above the dam where we'd had so much fun, all the summer. The Devon's course was determined by some familiar hills a little inland; it rose among highland farms and forests which we knew, passed at the end of its course through the school grounds, and then threw itself with little spectacle over a small waterfall beside the diving dam, and into the turbid Naguamsett.

The Devon School was astride these two rivers.

At the Crew House, Quackenbush, in the midst of some milling oarsmen in the damp main room, spotted me the instant I came in, with his dark expressionless eyes. Quackenbush was the crew manager, and there was something wrong about him. I didn't know exactly what it was. In the throng of the winter terms at Devon we were at opposite extremities of the class, and to me there only came the disliked edge of Quackenbush's reputation. A clue to it was that his first name was never used—I didn't even know what it was—and he had no nickname, not even an unfriendly one.

"Late, Forrester," he said in his already-matured voice. He was a firmly masculine type; perhaps he was disliked only because he had matured before the rest of us.

"Yes, sorry, I got held up."

"The crew waits for no man." He didn't seem to

think this was a funny thing to say. I did, and had to chuckle.

"Well, if you think it's all a joke . . ."

"I didn't say it was a joke."

"I've got to have some real help around here. This crew is going to win the New England scholastics, or my name isn't Cliff Quackenbush."

With that blank filled, I took up my duties as assistant senior crew manager. There is no such position officially, but it sometimes came into existence through necessity, and was the opposite of a sinecure. It was all work and no advantages. The official assistant to the crew manager was a member of the class below, and the following year he could come into the senior managership with its rights and status. An assistant who was already a senior ranked nowhere. Since I had applied for such a nonentity of a job, Quackenbush, who had known as little about me as I had about him, knew now.

"Get some towels," he said without looking at me, pointing at a door.

"How many?"

"Who knows? Get some. As many as you can carry. *That* won't be too many."

Jobs like mine were usually taken by boys with some physical disability, since everyone had to take part in sports and this was all disabled boys could do. As I walked toward the door I supposed that Quackenbush was studying me to see if he could detect a limp. But I knew that his flat black eyes would never detect my trouble.

Quackenbush felt mellower by the end of the afternoon as we stood on the float in front of the Crew House, gathering up towels.

"You never rowed did you." He opened the conversation like that, without pause or question mark. His voice sounded almost too mature, as though he were putting it on a little; he sounded as though he were speaking through a tube.

"No, I never did."

"I rowed on the lightweight crew for two years."

He had a tough bantam body, easily detectable under the tight sweat shirt he wore. "I wrestle in the winter," he went on. "What are you doing in the winter?"

"I don't know, manage something else."

"You're a senior aren't you?"

He knew that I was a senior. "Yeah."

"Starting a little late to manage teams aren't you?"

"Am I?"

"Damn right you are!" He put indignant conviction into this, pouncing on the first sprig of assertiveness in me.

"Well, it doesn't matter."

"Yes it matters."

"I don't think it does."

"Go to hell Forrester. Who the hell are you anyway."

I turned with an inward groan to look at him. Quackenbush wasn't going to let me just do the work for him like the automaton I wished to be. We were going to have to be pitted against each other. It was easy enough now to see why. For Quackenbush had been systematically disliked since he first set foot in Devon, with careless, disinterested insults coming at him from the beginning, voting for and applauding the class leaders through years of attaining nothing he wanted for himself. I didn't want to add to his humiliations; I even sympathized with his trembling, goaded egotism he could no longer contain, the furious arrogance which sprang out now at the mere hint of opposition from someone he had at last found whom he could consider inferior to himself. I realized that all this explained him, and it wasn't the words he said which angered me. It was only that he was so ignorant, that he knew nothing of the gypsy summer, nothing of the loss I was fighting to endure, of skylarks and splashes and petal-bearing breezes, he had not seen Leper's snails or the Charter of the Super Suicide Society; he shared nothing, knew nothing, felt nothing as Phineas had done.

"You, Quackenbush, don't know anything about who I am." That launched me, and I had to go on and say, "or anything else."

"Listen you maimed son-of-a-bitch . . ."

I hit him hard across the face. I didn't know why for an instant; it was almost as though I were maimed. Then the realization that there was someone who was flashed over me.

Quackenbush had clamped his arm in some kind of tight wrestling grip around my neck, and I was glad in this moment not to be a cripple. I reached over, grasped the back of his sweat shirt, wrenched, and it came away in my hand. I tried to throw him off, he lunged at the same time, and we catapulted into the water.

The dousing extinguished Quackenbush's rage, and he let go of me. I scrambled back onto the float, still seared by what he had said. "The next time you call anybody maimed," I bit off the words harshly so he would understand all of them, "you better make sure they are first."

"Get out of here, Forrester," he said bitterly from the water, "you're not wanted around here, Forrester. Get out of here."

I fought that battle, that first skirmish of a long campaign, for Finny. Until the back of my hand cracked against Quackenbush's face I had never pictured myself in the role of Finny's defender, and I didn't suppose that he would have thanked me for it now. He was too loyal to anything connected with himself—his roommate, his dormitory, his class, his school, outward in vastly expanded circles of loyalty until I couldn't imagine who would be excluded. But it didn't feel exactly as though I had done it for Phineas. It felt as though I had done it for myself.

If so I had little profit to show as I straggled back toward the dormitory dripping wet, with the job I had wanted gone, temper gone, mind circling over and over through the whole soured afternoon. I knew now that it was fall all right; I could feel it pressing clammily against my wet clothes, an unfriendly, discomforting breath in the air, an edge of wintery chill, air that shriveled, soon to put out the lights on the countryside. One of my legs wouldn't stop trembling, whether from cold or anger I couldn't tell. I wished I had hit him harder.

Someone was coming toward me along the bent, broken lane which led to the dormitory, a lane out of old London, ancient houses on either side leaning as though soon to tumble into it, cobblestones heaving underfoot like a bricked-over ocean squall—a figure of great height advanced down them toward me. It could only be Mr. Ludsbury; no one else could pass over these stones with such contempt for the idea of tripping.

The houses on either side were inhabited by I didn't know who; wispy, fragile old ladies seemed most likely. I couldn't duck into one of them. There were angles and bumps and bends everywhere, but none big enough to conceal me. Mr. Ludsbury loomed on like a high-masted clipper ship in this rocking passage, and I tried to go stealthily by him on my watery, squeaking sneakers.

"Just one moment, Forrester, if you please." Mr. Ludsbury's voice was bass, British, and his Adam's apple seemed to move as much as his mouth when he spoke. "Has there been a cloudburst in your part of town?"

"No, sir. I'm sorry, sir, I fell into the river." I apologized by instinct to him for this mishap which discomforted only me.

"And could you tell me how and why you fell into the river?"

"I slipped."

"Yes." After a pause he went on. "I think you have slipped in any number of ways since last year. I understand for example that there was gaming in my dormitory this summer while you were living there." He was in charge of the dormitory; one of the dispensations of those days of deliverance, I realized now, had been his absence.

"Gaming? What kind of gaming, sir?"

"Cards, dice," he shook his long hand dismissingly, "I didn't inquire. It didn't matter. There won't be any more of it."

"I don't know who that would have been." Nights of black-jack and poker and unpredictable games invented by Phineas rose up in my mind; the back room of Leper's suite, a lamp hung with a blanket so that only a small blazing circle of light fell sharply amid the surrounding darkness; Phineas losing even in those games he invented, betting always for what *should* win, for what would have been the most brilliant successes of all, if only the cards hadn't betrayed him.

Finny finally betting his icebox and losing it, that contraption, to me.

I thought of it because Mr. Ludsbury was just then saying, "And while I'm putting the dormitory back together I'd better tell you to get rid of that leaking icebox. Nothing like that is ever permitted in the dormitory, of course. I notice that everything went straight to seed during the summer and that none of you old boys who knew our standards so much as lifted a finger to help Mr. Prud'homme maintain order. As a substitute for the summer he couldn't have been expected to know everything there was to be known at once. You old boys simply took advantage of the situation."

I stood there shaking in my wet sneakers. If only I had truly taken advantage of the situation, seized and held and prized the multitudes of advantages the summer offered me; if only I had.

I said nothing, on my face I registered the bleak look of a defendant who knows the court will never be swayed by all the favorable evidence he has. It was a schoolboy look; Mr. Ludsbury knew it well.

"There's a long-distance call for you," he continued in the tone of the judge performing the disagreeable duty of telling the defendant his right. "I've written the operator's number on the pad beside the telephone in my study. You may go in and call."

"Thank you very much, sir."

He sailed on down the lane without further reference to me, and I wondered who was sick at home.

But when I reached his study—low-ceilinged, gloomy with books, black leather chairs, a pipe rack, frayed brown rug, a room which students rarely entered except for a reprimand—I saw on the pad not an operator's number from my home town, but one which seemed to interrupt the beating of my heart.

I called this operator, and listened in wonder while she went through her routine as though this were just any long-distance call, and then her voice left the line and it was pre-empted, and charged, by the voice of Phineas. "Happy first day of the new academic year!"

"Thanks, thanks a lot, it's a—you sound—I'm glad to hear your—"

"Stop stuttering, I'm paying for this. Who're you rooming with?"

"Nobody. They didn't put anyone else in the room."

"Saving my place for me! Good old Devon. But anyway, you wouldn't have let them put anyone else in there, would you?" Friendliness, simple outgoing affection, that was all I could hear in his voice.

"No, of course not."

"I didn't think you would. Roommates are roommates. Even if they do have an occasional fight. God you were crazy when you were here."

"I guess I was. I guess I must have been."

"Completely over the falls. I wanted to be sure you'd recovered. That's why I called up. I knew that if you'd let them put anybody else in the room in my place, then you really *were* crazy. But you didn't, I knew you wouldn't. Well, I did have just a *trace* of doubt, that was because you talked so crazy here. I have to admit I had just a *second* when I wondered. I'm sorry about that, Gene. Naturally I was completely wrong. You didn't let them put anyone else in my spot."

"No, I didn't let them."

"I could shoot myself for thinking you might. I really knew you wouldn't."

"No, I wouldn't."

"And I spent my money on a long-distance call! All

for nothing. Well, it's spent, on you too. So start talking, pal. And it better be good. Start with sports. What are you going out for?"

"Crew. Well, not exactly crew. Managing crew. Assistant crew manager."

"Assistant _crew_ manager!"

"I don't think I've got the job—"

"Assistant crew _manager!_"

"I got in a fight this after—"

"_Assistant crew manager!_" No voice could course with dumfoundment like Finny's "You _are_ crazy!"

"Listen, Finny, I don't care about being a big man on the campus or anything."

"Whaaat?" Much more clearly than anything in Mr. Ludsbury's study I could see his face now, grimacing in wide, obsessed stupefaction. "Who said anything about whoever _they_ are!"

"Well then what are you so worked up for?"

"What do you want to manage crew for? What do you want to _manage_ for? What's that got to do with sports?"

The point was, the grace of it was, that it had nothing to do with sports. For I wanted no more of sports. They were barred from me, as though when Dr. Stanpole said, "Sports are finished" he had been speaking of me. I didn't trust myself in them, and I didn't trust anyone else. It was as though football players were really bent on crushing the life out of each other, as though boxers were in combat to the death, as though even a tennis ball might turn into a bullet. This didn't seem completely crazy imagination in 1942, when jumping out of trees stood for abandoning a torpedoed ship. Later, in the school swimming pool, we were given the second stage in that rehearsal: after you hit the water you made big splashes with your hands, to scatter the flaming oil which would be on the surface.

So to Phineas I said, "I'm too busy for sports," and he went into his incoherent groans and jumbles of words, and I thought the issue was settled until at the end he said, "Listen, pal, if *I* can't play sports, *you're* going to play them for me," and I lost part of myself to him then, and a soaring sense of freedom revealed that this must have been my purpose from the first: to become a part of Phineas.

7

Brinker Hadley came across to see me late that afternoon. I had taken a shower to wash off the sticky salt of the Naguamsett River—going into the Devon was like taking a refreshing shower itself, you never had to clean up after it, but the Naguamsett was something else entirely. I had never been in it before; it seemed appropriate that my baptism there had taken place on the first day of this winter session, and that I had been thrown into it, in the middle of a fight.

I washed the traces off me and then put on a pair of chocolate brown slacks, a pair which Phineas had been particularly critical of when he wasn't wearing them, and a blue flannel shirt. Then, with nothing to do until my French class at five o'clock, I began turning over in my mind this question of sports.

But Brinker came in. I think he made a point of visiting all the rooms near him the first day. "Well, Gene," his beaming face appeared around the door. Brinker looked the standard preparatory school article in his gray gabardine suit with square, hand-sewn-looking jacket pockets, a conservative necktie, and dark brown cordovan shoes. His face was all straight lines—eyebrows, mouth, nose, everything—and he carried his six feet of height straight as well. He looked but happened not to be athletic, being too busy with politics, arrangements, and offices. There was nothing idiosyncratic about Brinker unless you saw him from behind; I did as he turned to close the door after him. The flaps of his gabardine jacket parted slightly over his healthy rump, and it is that, without any sense of derision at all, that I recall as Brinker's salient characteristic, those healthy, determined, not over-exaggerated but definite and substantial buttocks.

"Here you are in your solitary splendor," he went on genially. "I can see you have real influence around here. This big room all to yourself. I wish I knew how to manage things like you." He grinned confidingly and sank down on my cot, leaning on his elbow in a relaxed, at-home way.

It didn't seem fitting for Brinker Hadley, the hub of the class, to be congratulating me on influence. I was going to say that while he had a roommate it was frightened Brownie Perkins, who would never impinge on Brinker's comfort in any way, and that they had two rooms, the front one with a fireplace. Not that I grudged him any of this. I liked Brinker in spite of his Winter Session efficiency; almost everyone liked Brinker.

But in the pause I took before replying he started talking in his lighthearted way again. He never let a dull spot appear in conversation if he could help it.

"I'll bet you knew all the time Finny wouldn't be back this fall. That's why you picked him for a roommate, right?"

"What?" I pulled quickly around in my chair, away from the desk, and faced him. "No, of course not. How could I know a thing like that in advance?"

Brinker glanced swiftly at me. "You fixed it," he

smiled widely. "You knew all the time. I'll bet it was *all* your doing."

"Don't be nutty, Brinker," I turned back toward the desk and began moving books with rapid pointlessness, "what a crazy thing to say." My voice sounded too strained even to my own blood-pounded ears.

"Ah-h-h. The truth hurts, eh?"

I looked at him as sharply as eyes can look. He had struck an accusing pose.

"Sure," I gave a short laugh, "sure." Then these words came out of me by themselves, "But the truth will out."

His hand fell leadenly on my shoulder. "Rest assured of that, my son. In our free democracy, even fighting for its life, the truth will out."

I got up. "I feel like a smoke, don't you? Let's go down to the Butt Room."

"Yes, yes. To the dungeon with you."

The Butt Room was something like a dungeon. It was in the basement, or the bowels, of the dormitory. There were about ten smokers already there. Everyone at Devon had many public faces; in class we looked, if not exactly scholarly, at least respectably alert; on the playing fields we looked like innocent extroverts; and in the Butt Room we looked, very strongly, like criminals. The school's policy, in order to discourage smoking, was to make these rooms as depressing as possible. The windows near the ceiling were small and dirty, the old leather furniture spilled its inwards, the tables were mutilated, the walls ash-colored, the floor concrete. A radio with a faulty connection played loud and rasping for a while, then suddenly quiet and insinuating.

"Here's your prisoner, gentlemen," announced Brinker, seizing my neck and pushing me into the

Butt Room ahead of him, "I'm turning him over to the proper authorities."

High spirits came hard in the haze of the Butt Room. A slumped figure near the radio, which happened to be playing loud at the moment, finally roused himself to say, "What's the charge?"

"Doing away with his roommate so he could have a whole room to himself. Rankest treachery." He paused impressively. "Practically fratricide."

With a snap of the neck I shook his hand off me, my teeth set, "Brinker . . ."

He raised an arresting hand. "Not a word. Not a sound. You'll have your day in court."

"God damn it! Shut up! I swear to God you ride a joke longer than anybody I know."

It was a mistake; the radio had suddenly gone quiet, and my voice ringing in the abrupt, releasing hush galvanized them all.

"So, you killed him, did you?" A boy uncoiled tensely from the couch.

"Well," Brinker qualified judiciously, "not actually killed. Finny's hanging between life and death at home, in the arms of his grief-stricken old mother."

I had to take part in this, or risk losing control completely. "I didn't do hardly a thing," I began as easily as it was possible for me to do, "I—all I did was drop a little bit . . . a little pinch of arsenic in his morning coffee."

"Liar!" Brinker glowered at me. "Trying to weasel out of it with a false confession, eh?"

I laughed at that, laughed uncontrollably for a moment at that.

"We know the scene of the crime," Brinker went on, "high in that . . . that *funereal* tree by the river. There wasn't any poison, nothing as subtle as that."

"Oh, you know about the tree," I tried to let my face fall guiltily, but it felt instead as though it were being dragged downward. "Yes, huh, yes there was a small, a little *contretemps* at the tree."

No one was diverted from the issue by this try at a funny French pronunciation.

"Tell us everything," a younger boy at the table said huskily. There was an unsettling current in his voice, a genuinely conspiratorial note, as though he believed literally everything that had been said. His attitude seemed to me almost obscene, the attitude of someone who discovers a sexual secret of yours and promises not to tell a soul if you will describe it in detail to him.

"Well," I replied in a stronger voice, "first I stole all his money. Then I found that he cheated on his entrance tests to Devon and I blackmailed his parents about that, then I made love to his sister in Mr. Ludsbury's study, then I . . ." it was going well, faint grins were appearing around the room, even the younger boy seemed to suspect that he was being "sincere" about a joke, a bad mistake to make at Devon, "then I . . ." I only had to add, "pushed him out of the tree" and the chain of implausibility would be complete, "then I . . ." just those few words and perhaps this dungeon nightmare would end.

But I could feel my throat closing on them; I could never say them, never.

I swung on the younger boy. "What did I do then?" I demanded. "I'll bet you've got a lot of theories. Come on, reconstruct the crime. There we were at the tree. Then what happened, Sherlock Holmes?"

His eyes swung guiltily back and forth. "Then you just pushed him off, I'll bet."

"Lousy bet," I said offhandedly, falling into a chair

as though losing interest in the game. "You lose. I guess you're Dr. Watson, after all."

They laughed at him a little, and he squirmed and looked guiltier than ever. He had a very weak foothold among the Butt Room crowd, and I had pretty well pushed him off it. His glance flickered out at me from his defeat, and I saw to my surprise that I had, by making a little fun of him, brought upon myself his unmixed hatred. For my escape this was a price I was willing to pay.

"French, French," I exclaimed. "Enough of this *contretemps*. I've got to study my French." And I went out.

Going up the stairs I heard a voice from the Butt Room say, "Funny, he came all the way down here and didn't even have a smoke."

But this was a clue they soon seemed to forget. I detected no Sherlock Holmes among them, nor even a Dr. Watson. No one showed any interest in tracking me, no one pried, no one insinuated. The daily lists of appointments lengthened with the rays of the receding autumn sun until the summer, the opening day, even yesterday became by the middle of October something gotten out of the way and forgotten, because tomorrow bristled with so much to do.

In addition to classes and sports and clubs, there was the war. Brinker Hadley could compose his Shortest War Poem Ever Written

> The War
> Is a bore

if he wanted to, but all of us had to take stronger action than that. First there was the local apple crop, threatening to rot because the harvesters had all gone

into the army or war factories. We spent several shining days picking them and were paid in cash for it.
Brinker was inspired to write his Apple Ode

> Our chore
> Is the core
> of the war

and the novelty and money of these days excited us.
Life at Devon was revealed as still very close to the
ways of peace; the war was at worst only a bore, as
Brinker said, no more taxing to us than a day spent
at harvesting in an apple orchard.

Not long afterward, early even for New Hampshire,
snow came. It came theatrically, late one afternoon;
I looked up from my desk and saw that suddenly there
were big flakes twirling down into the quadrangle,
settling on the carefully pruned shrubbery bordering
the crosswalks, the three elms still holding many of
their leaves, the still-green lawns. They gathered there
thicker by the minute, like noiseless invaders conquering because they took possession so gently. I watched
them whirl past my window—don't take this seriously,
the playful way they fell seemed to imply, this little
show, this harmless trick.

It seemed to be true. The school was thinly blanketed that night, but the next morning, a bright, almost
balmy day, every flake disappeared. The following
weekend, however, it snowed again, then two days
later much harder, and by the end of that week the
ground had been clamped under snow for the winter.

In the same way the war, beginning almost humorously with announcements about maids and days spent
at apple-picking, commenced its invasion of the school.
The early snow was commandeered as its advance
guard.

Leper Lepellier didn't suspect this. It was not in fact evident to anyone at first. But Leper stands out for me as the person who was most often and most emphatically taken by surprise, by this and every other shift in our life at Devon.

The heavy snow paralyzed the railroad yards of one of the large towns south of us on the Boston and Maine line. At chapel the day following the heaviest snowfall, two hundred volunteers were solicited to spend the day shoveling them out, as part of the Emergency Usefulness policy adopted by the faculty that fall. Again we would be paid. So we all volunteered, Brinker and I and Chet Douglass and even I noticed, Quackenbush.

But not Leper. He generally made little sketches of birds and trees in the back of his notebook during chapel, so that he had probably not heard the announcement. The train to take us south to the work did not arrive until after lunch, and on my way to the station, taking a short cut through a meadow not far from the river, I met Leper. I had hardly seen him all fall, and I hardly recognized him now. He was standing motionless on the top of a small ridge, and he seemed from a distance to be a scarecrow left over from the growing season. As I plodded toward him through the snow I began to differentiate items of clothing—a dull green deer-stalker's cap, brown ear muffs, a thick gray woolen scarf—then at last I recognified the face in the midst of them, Leper's, pinched and pink, his eyes peering curiously toward some distant woods through steel-rimmed glasses. As I got nearer I noticed that below his long tan canvas coat with sagging pockets, below the red and black plaid woolen knickers and green puttees, he was wearing skis. They were very long, wooden and battered, and had two decorative, old-fashioned knobs on their tips.

"You think there's a path through those woods?" he asked in his mild tentative voice when I got near. Leper did not switch easily from one train of thought to another, and even though I was an old friend whom he had not talked to in months I didn't mind his taking me for granted now, even at this improbable meeting in a wide, empty field of snow.

"I'm not sure, Leper, but I think there's one at the bottom of the slope."

"Oh yeah, I guess there is." We always called him Leper to his face; he wouldn't have remembered to respond to any other name.

I couldn't keep from staring at him, at the burlesque explorer look of him. "What are you," I asked at last, "um, what are you doing, anyway?"

"I'm touring."

"Touring." I examined the long bamboo ski poles he held. "How do you mean, touring?"

"Touring. It's the way you get around the country-side in the winter. Touring skiing. It's how you go overland in the snow."

"Where are you going?"

"Well, I'm not *going* anywhere." He bent down to tighten the lacings on a puttee. "I'm just touring around."

"There's that place across the river where you could ski. The place where they have the rope tow on that steep hill across from the railroad station. You could go over there."

"No, I don't think so." He surveyed the woods again, although his breath had fogged his glasses. "That's not skiing."

"Why sure that's skiing. It's a good little run, you can get going pretty fast on that hill."

"Yeah but that's it, that's why it isn't skiing. Skiing isn't supposed to be fast. Skis are for useful locomotion." He turned his inquiring eyes on me. "You can break a leg with that downhill stuff."

"Not on that little hill."

"Well, it's the same thing. It's part of the whole wrong idea. They're ruining skiing in this country, rope tows and chair lifts and all that stuff. You get carted up, and then you whizz down. You never get to see the trees or anything. Oh you see a lot of trees shoot by, but you never get to really look at trees, at a tree. I just like to go along and see what I'm passing and enjoy myself." He had come to the end of his thought, and now he slowly took me in, noticing my layers of old clothes. "What are you doing, anyway?" he asked mildly and curiously.

"Going to work on the railroad." He kept gazing mildly and curiously at me. "Shovel out those tracks. That work they talked about in chapel this morning. You remember."

"Have a nice day at it, anyway," he said.

"I will. You too."

"I will if I find what I'm looking for—a beaver dam. It used to be up the Devon a ways, in a little stream that flows into the Devon. It's interesting to see the way beavers adapt to the winter. Have you ever seen it?"

"No, I never have seen that."

"Well, you might want to come sometime, if I find the place."

"Tell me if you find it."

With Leper it was always a fight, a hard fight to win when you were seventeen years old and lived in a keyed-up, competing school, to avoiding making fun

of him. But as I had gotten to know him better this
fight had been easier to win.

Shoving in his long bamboo poles he pushed deliberately forward and slid slowly away from me down
the gradual slope, standing very upright, his skis far
apart to guard against any threat to his balance, his
poles sticking out on either side of him, as though to
ward off any interference.

I turned and trudged off to help shovel out New
England for the war.

We spent an odd day, toiling in that railroad yard.
By the time we arrived there the snow had become
drab and sooted, wet and heavy. We were divided
into gangs, each under an old railroad man. Brinker,
Chet and I managed to be in the same group, but the
playful atmosphere of the apple orchard was gone. Of
the town we could only see some dull red brick mills
and warehouses surrounding the yards, and we labored
away among what the old man directing us called
"rolling stock"—grim freight cars from many parts of
the country immobilized in the snow. Brinker asked
him if it shouldn't be called "unrolling stock" now,
and the old man looked back at him with bleary dislike and didn't reply. Nothing was very funny that day,
the work became hard and unvarying; I began to
sweat under my layers of clothes. By the middle of the
afternoon we had lost our fresh volunteer look, the
grime of the railroad and the exhaustion of manual
laborers were on us all; we seemed of a piece with the
railroad yards and the mills and warehouses. The old
man resented us, or we made him nervous, or maybe
he was as sick as he looked. For whatever reason he
grumbled and spat and alternated between growling
orders and rubbing his big, unhealthy belly.

Around 4:30 there was a moment of cheer. The main

line had been cleared and the first train rattled slowly through. We watched it advance toward us, the engine throwing up balls of steam to add to the heavy overcast.

All of us lined both sides of the track and got ready to cheer the engineer and passengers. The coach windows were open and the passengers surprisingly were hanging out; they were all men, I could discern, all young, all alike. It was a troop train.

Over the clatter and banging of the wheels and couplings we cheered and they yelled back, both sides taken by surprise. They were not much older than we were and although probably just recruits, they gave the impression of being an elite as they were carried past our drab ranks. They seemed to be having a wonderful time, their uniforms looked new and good; they were clean and energetic; they were going places.

After they had gone we laborers looked rather emptily across the newly cleared rails at each other, at ourselves, and not even Brinker thought of the timely remark. We turned away. The old man told us to go back to other parts of the yard, but there was no more real work done that afternoon. Stranded in this mill town railroad yard while the whole world was converging elsewhere, we seemed to be nothing but children playing among heroic men.

The day ended at last. Gray from the beginning, its end was announced by a deepening gray, of sky, snow, faces, spirits. We piled back into the old, dispiritedly lit coaches waiting for us, slumped into the uncomfortable green seats, and no one said much until we were miles away.

When we did speak it was about aviation training programs and brothers in the service and requirements for enlistment and the futility of Devon and how we

would never have war stories to tell our grandchildren
and how long the war might last and who ever heard
of studying dead languages at a time like this.

Quackenbush took advantage of a break in this line
of conversation to announce that he would certainly
stay at Devon through the year, however half-cocked
others might rush off. He elaborated without encour-
agement, citing the advantages of Devon's physical
hardening program and of a high school diploma when
he did in good time reach basic training. He for one
would advance into the army step by step.

"You for one," echoed someone contemptuously.

"You *are* one," someone else said.

"Which army, Quackenbush? Mussolini's?"

"Naw, he's a Kraut."

"He's a Kraut spy."

"How many rails did you sabotage today, Quackenbush?"

"I thought they interned all Quackenbushes the day
after Pearl Harbor."

To which Brinker added: "They didn't find him. He
hid his light under a Quackenbush."

We were all tired at the end of that day.

Walking back to the school grounds from the railroad station in the descending darkness we overtook
a lone figure sliding along the snow-covered edge of
the street.

"Will you look at Lepellier," began Brinker irritably.
"Who does he think he is, the Abominable Snowman?"

"He's just been out skiing around," I said quickly. I
didn't want to see today's strained tempers exploding
on Leper. Then as we came up beside him, "Did you
find the dam, Leper?"

He turned his head slowly, without breaking his
forward movement of alternately planted poles and

thrust skis, rhythmically but feebly continuous like a homemade piston engine's. "You know what? I did find it," his smile was wide and unfocused, as though not for me alone but for anyone and anything which wished to share this pleasure with him, "and it was really interesting to see. I took some pictures of it, and if they come out I'll bring them over and show you."

"What dam is that?" Brinker asked me.

"It's a . . . well a little dam up the river he knows about," I said.

"I don't know of any dam up the river."

"Well, it's not in the Devon itself, it's in one of the . . . tributaries."

"Tributaries! To the *Devon?*"

"You know, a little creek or something."

He knit his brows in mystification. "What kind of a dam is this, anyway?"

"Well," he couldn't be put off with half a story, "it's a beaver dam."

Brinker's shoulders fell under the weight of this news. "That's the kind of a place I'm in with a world war going on. A school for photographers of beaver dams."

"The beaver never appeared himself," Leper offered.

Brinker turned elaborately toward him. "Didn't he really?"

"No. But I guess I was pretty clumsy getting close to it, so he might have heard me and been frightened."

"Well." Brinker's expansive, dazed tone suggested that here was one of life's giant ironies, "There you are!"

"Yes," agreed Leper after a thoughtful pause, "there you are."

"Here we are," I said, pulling Brinker around the

corner we had reached which led to our dormitory. "So long, Leper. Glad you found it."

"Oh," he raised his voice after us, "how was your day? How did the work go?"

"Just like a stag at eve," Brinker roared back. "It was a winter wonderland, every minute." And out of the side of his mouth, to me, "Everybody in this place is either a draft-dodging Kraut or a . . . a . . ." the scornful force of his tone turned the word into a curse, "a *nat-u-ral-ist!*" He grabbed my arm agitatedly. "I'm giving it up, I'm going to enlist. Tomorrow."

I felt a thrill when he said it. This was the logical climax of the whole misbegotten day, this whole out-of-joint term at Devon. I think I had been waiting for a long time for someone to say this so that I could entertain these decisive words myself.

To enlist. To slam the door impulsively on the past, to shed everything down to my last bit of clothing, to break the pattern of my life—that complex design I had been weaving since birth with all its dark threads, its unexplainable symbols set against a conventional background of domestic white and schoolboy blue, all those tangled strands which required the dexterity of a virtuoso to keep flowing—I yearned to take giant military shears to it, snap! bitten off in an instant, and nothing left in my hands but spools of khaki which could weave only a plain, flat, khaki design, however twisted they might be.

Not that it would be a good life. The war would be deadly all right. But I was used to finding something deadly in things that attracted me; there was always something deadly lurking in anything I wanted, anything I loved. And if it wasn't there, as for example with Phineas, then I put it there myself.

But in the war, there was no question about it at all; it was there.

I separated from Brinker in the quadrangle, since one of his clubs was meeting and he could not go back to the dormitory yet—"I've got to preside at a meeting of the Golden Fleece Debating Society tonight," he said in a tone of amazed contempt, "the Golden Fleece Debating Society! We're mad here, all mad," and he went off raving to himself in the dark.

It was a night made for hard thoughts. Sharp stars pierced singly through the blackness, not sweeps of them or clusters or Milky Ways as there might have been in the South, but single, chilled points of light, as unromantic as knife blades. Devon, muffled under the gentle occupation of the snow, was dominated by them; the cold Yankee stars ruled this night. They did not invoke in me thoughts of God, or sailing before the mast, or some great love as crowded night skies at home had done; I thought instead, in the light of those cold points, of the decision facing me.

Why go through the motions of getting an education and watch the war slowly chip away at the one thing I had loved here, the peace, the measureless, careless peace of the Devon summer? Others, the Quackenbushes of this world, could calmly watch the war approach them and jump into it at the last and most advantageous instant, as though buying into the stock market. But I couldn't.

There was no one to stop me but myself. Putting aside soft reservations about What I Owed Devon and my duty to my parents and so on, I reckoned my responsibilities by the light of the unsentimental night sky and knew that I owed no one anything. I owed it to myself to meet this crisis in my life when I chose, and I chose now.

I bounced zestfully up the dormitory stairs. Perhaps because my mind still retained the image of the sharp night stars, those few fixed points of light in the darkness, perhaps because of that the warm yellow light streaming from under my own door came as such a shock. It was a simple case of a change of expectation. The light should have been off. Instead, as though alive itself, it poured in a thin yellow slab of brightness from under the door, illuminating the dust and splinters of the hall floor.

I grabbed the knob and swung open the door. He was seated in my chair at the desk, bending down to adjust the gross encumbrance of his leg, so that only the familiar ears set close against his head were visible, and his short-cut brown hair. He looked up with a provocative grin, "Hi pal, where's the brass band?"

Everything that had happened throughout the day faded like that first false snowfall of the winter. Phineas was back.

8

"I can see I never should have left you alone," Phineas went on before I could recover from the impact of finding him there, "Where did you get *those* clothes!" His bright, indignant eyes swept from my battered gray cap, down the frayed sweater and paint-stained pants to a pair of clodhoppers. "You don't have to advertise like that, we all know you're the worst dressed man in the class."

"I've been working, that's all. These are just work clothes."

"In the boiler room?"

"On the railroad. Shoveling snow."

He sat back in the chair. "Shoveling railroad snow. Well that makes sense, we always did that the first term."

I pulled off the sweater, under which I was wearing a rain slicker I used to go sailing in, a kind of canvas sack. Phineas just studied it in wordless absorption. "I like the cut of it," he finally murmured. I pulled that off revealing an Army fatigue shirt my brother had given me. "Very topical," said Phineas through his teeth. After that came off there was just my undershirt, stained with sweat. He smiled at it for a while and then said as he heaved himself out of the chair,

"There. You should have worn that all day, just that. That has real taste. The rest of your outfit was just gilding that lily of a sweat shirt."

"Glad to hear you like it."

"Not at all," he replied ambiguously, reaching for a pair of crutches which leaned against the desk.

I took the sight of this all right, I had seen him on crutches the year before when he broke his ankle playing football. At Devon crutches had almost as many athletic associations as shoulder pads. And I had never seen an invalid whose skin glowed with such health, accenting the sharp clarity of his eyes, or one who used his arms and shoulders on crutches as though on parallel bars, as though he would do a somersault on them if he felt like it. Phineas vaulted across the room to his cot, yanked back the spread and then groaned. "Oh Christ, it's not made up. What is all this crap about no maids?"

"No maids," I said. "After all, there's a war on. It's not much of a sacrifice, when you think of people starving and being bombed and all the other things." My unselfishness was responding properly to the influences of 1942. In these past months Phineas and I had grown apart on this; I felt a certain disapproval of him for grumbling about a lost luxury, with a war on. "After all," I repeated, "there is a war on."

"Is there?" he murmured absently. I didn't pay any attention; he was always speaking when his thoughts were somewhere else, asking rhetorical questions and echoing other people's words.

I found some sheets and made up his bed for him. He wasn't a bit sensitive about being helped, not a bit like an invalid striving to seem independent. I put this on the list of things to include when I said some prayers, the first in a long time, that night in bed. Now that Phineas was back it seemed time to start saying prayers again.

After the lights went out the special quality of my silence let him know that I was saying them, and he kept quiet for approximately three minutes. Then he began to talk; he never went to sleep without talking first and he seemed to feel that prayers lasting more than three minutes were showing off. God was always unoccupied in Finny's universe, ready to lend an ear any time at all. Anyone who failed to get his message through in three minutes, as I sometimes failed to do when trying to impress him, Phineas, with my sanctity, wasn't trying.

He was still talking when I fell asleep, and the next morning, through the icy atmosphere which one window raised an inch had admitted to our room, he woke me with the overindignant shout, "What *is* all this crap about no maids!" He was sitting up in bed, as though ready to spring out of it, totally and energetically awake. I had to laugh at this indignant athlete, with the strength of five people, complaining about the service. He threw back his bedclothes and said, "Hand me my crutches, will you?"

Until now, in spite of everything, I had welcomed each new day as though it were a new life, where all past failures and problems were erased, and all future possibilities and joys open and available, to be achieved probably before night fell again. Now, in this winter of snow and crutches with Phineas, I began to know that each morning reasserted the problems of the night before, that sleep suspended all but changed nothing, that you couldn't make yourself over between dawn and dusk. Phineas however did not believe this. I'm sure that he looked down at his leg every morning first thing, as soon as he remembered it, to see if it had not been totally restored while he slept. When he found on this first morning back at Devon that it happened still to be crippled and in a cast, he said in his usual self-contained way, "Hand me my crutches, will you?"

Brinker Hadley, next door, always awoke like an express train. There was a gathering rumble through the wall, as Brinker reared up in bed, coughed hoarsely, slammed his feet on the floor, pounded through the freezing air to the closet for something in the way of clothes, and thundered down the hall to the bathroom. Today, however, he veered and broke into our room instead.

"Ready to sign up?" he shouted before he was through the door. "You ready to en—Finny!"

"You ready to en—what?" pursued Finny from his bed. "Who's ready to sign and en what?"

"Finny. By God you're back!"

"Sure," confirmed Finny with a slight, pleased grin.

"So," Brinker curled his lip at me, "your little plot didn't work so well after all."

"What's he talking about?" said Finny as I thrust his crutches beneath his shoulders.

"Just talking," I said shortly. "What does Brinker ever talk about?"

"*You* know what I'm talking about well enough."

"No I don't."

"Oh yes you do."

"Are you telling me what I know?"

"Damn right I am."

"What's he *talking* about," said Finny.

The room was bitterly cold. I stood trembling in front of Phineas, still holding his crutches in place, unable to turn and face Brinker and this joke he had gotten into his head, this catastrophic joke.

"He wants to know if I'll sign up with him," I said, "enlist." It was the ultimate question for all seventeen-year-olds that year, and it drove Brinker's insinuations from every mind but mine.

"Yeah," said Brinker.

"Enlist!" cried Finny at the same time. His large and clear eyes turned with an odd expression on me. I had never seen such a look in them before. After looking at me closely he said, "You're going to enlist?"

"Well I just thought—last night after the railroad work—"

"You thought you might sign up?" he went on, looking carefully away.

Brinker drew one of his deep senatorial breaths, but he found nothing to say. We three stood shivering in the thin New Hampshire morning light, Finny and I in pajamas, Brinker in a blue flannel bathrobe and ripped moccasins. "When will you?" Finny went on.

"Oh, I don't know," I said. "It was just something Brinker happened to say last night, that's all."

"I said," Brinker began in an unusually guarded voice, glancing quickly at Phineas, "I said something about enlisting today."

Finny hobbled over to the dresser and took up his soap dish. "I'm first in the shower," he said.

"You can't get that cast wet, can you?" asked Brinker.

"No, I'll keep it outside the curtain."

"I'll help," said Brinker.

"No," said Finny without looking at him, "I can manage all right."

"How can you manage all right?" Brinker persisted aggressively.

"I can *manage* all right," Finny repeated with a set face.

I could hardly believe it, but it was too plainly

printed in the closed expression of his face to mistake, too discernible beneath the even tone of his voice: Phineas was shocked at the idea of my leaving. In some way he needed me. He needed me. I was the least trustworthy person he had ever met. I knew that; he knew or should know that too. I had even told him. I had told him. But there was no mistaking the shield of remoteness in his face and voice. He wanted me around. The war then passed away from me, and dreams of enlistment and escape and a clean start lost their meaning for me.

"Sure you can manage the shower all right," I said, "but what difference does it make? Come on. Brinker's always . . . Brinker's always getting there first. Enlist! What a nutty idea. It's just Brinker wanting to get there first again. I wouldn't enlist with you if you were General MacArthur's eldest son."

Brinker reared back arrogantly. "And who do you think I am!" But Finny hadn't heard that. His face had broken into a wide and dazzled smile at what I had said, lighting up his whole face. "Enlist!" I drove on, "I wouldn't enlist with you if you were Elliott Roosevelt."

"First cousin," said Brinker over his chin, "once removed."

"He wouldn't enlist with you," Finny plunged in, "if you were Madame Chiang Kai-shek."

"Well," I qualified in an undertone, "he really *is* Madame Chiang Kai-shek."

"Well fan my brow," cried Finny, giving us his stunned look of total appalled horrified amazement, "who would have thought that! Chinese. The Yellow Peril, right here at Devon."

And as far as the history of the Class of 1943 at the Devon School is concerned, this was the only part of our conversation worth preserving. Brinker Hadley had been tagged with a nickname at last, after four years of creating them for others and eluding one himself. "Yellow Peril" Hadley swept through the school with the speed of a flu epidemic, and it must be said to his credit that Brinker took it well enough except when, in its inevitable abbreviation, people sometimes called him "Yellow" instead of "Peril."

But in a week I had forgotten that, and I have never since forgotten the dazed look on Finny's face when he thought that on the first day of his return to Devon I was going to desert him. I didn't know why he had chosen me, why it was only to me that he could show the most humbling sides of his handicap. I didn't care. For the war was no longer eroding the peaceful summertime stillness I had prized so much at Devon, and although the playing fields were crusted under a foot of congealed snow and the river was now a hard gray-white lane of ice between gaunt trees, peace had come back to Devon for me.

So the war swept over like a wave at the seashore, gathering power and size as it bore on us, overwhelming in its rush, seemingly inescapable, and then at the last moment eluded by a word from Phineas; I had simply ducked, that was all, and the wave's concentrated power had hurtled harmlessly overhead, no doubt throwing others roughly up on the beach, but leaving me peaceably treading water as before. I did not stop to think that one wave is inevitably followed by another even larger and more powerful, when the tide is coming in.

"I *like* the winter," Finny assured me for the fourth time, as we came back from chapel that morning.

"Well, it doesn't like you." Wooden plank walks had

been placed on many of the school paths for better footing, but there were icy patches everywhere on them. A crutch misplaced and he could be thrown down upon the frozen wooden planking, or into the ice-encrusted snow.

Even indoors Devon was a nest of traps for him. The school had been largely rebuilt with a massive bequest from an oil family some years before in a peculiar style of Puritan grandeur, as though Versailles had been modified for the needs of a Sunday school. This opulent sobriety betrayed the divided nature of the school, just as in a different way the two rivers that it straddled did. From the outside the buildings were reticent, severe straight lines of red brick or white clapboard, with shutters standing sentinel beside each window, and a few unassuming white cupolas placed here and there on the roofs because they were expected and not pretty, like Pilgrim bonnets.

But once you passed through the Colonial doorways, with only an occasional fan window or low relief pillar to suggest that a certain muted adornment was permissible, you entered an extravaganza of Pompadour splendor. Pink marble walls and white marble floors were enclosed by arched and vaulted ceilings; an assembly room had been done in the manner of the High Italian Renaissance, another was illuminated by chandeliers flashing with crystal teardrops; there was a wall of fragile French windows overlooking an Italian garden of marble bric-à-brac; the library was Provençal on the first floor, rococo on the second. And everywhere, except in the dormitories, the floors and stairs were of smooth, slick marble, more treacherous even than the icy walks.

"The winter loves me," he retorted, and then, disliking the whimsical sound of that, added, "I mean as much as you can say a season can love. What I mean is, I love winter, and when you really love something, then it loves you back, in whatever way it has to love." I didn't think that this was true, my seventeen years of experience had shown this to be much more false than true, but it was like every other thought and belief of Finny's: it should have been true. So I didn't argue.

The board walk ended and he moved a little ahead of me as we descended a sloping path toward our first class. He picked his way with surprising care, surprising in anyone who before had used the ground mainly as a point of departure, as the given element in a suspended world of leaps in space. And now I remembered what I had never taken any special note of before: how Phineas used to walk. Around Devon we had gaits of every description; gangling shuffles from boys who had suddenly grown a foot taller, swinging cowboy lopes from those thinking of how wide their shoulders had become, ambles, waddles, light trippings, gigantic Bunyan strides. But Phineas had moved in continuous flowing balance, so that he had seemed to drift along with no effort at all, relaxation on the move. He hobbled now among the patches of ice. There was the one certainty that Dr. Stanpole had given—Phineas would walk again. But the thought was there before me that he would never walk like that again.

"Do you have a class?" he said as we reached the steps of the building.

"Yes."

"So do I. Let's not go."

"Not go? But what'll we use for an excuse?"

"We'll say I fainted from exertion on the way from

chapel," he looked at me with a phantom's smile, "and you had to tend me."

"This is your first day back, Finny. You're no one to cut classes."

"I know, I know. I'm going to work. I really am going to work. You're going to pull me through mostly, but I *am* going to work as hard as I can. Only not today, not the first thing. *Not* now, not conjugating verbs when I haven't even looked at the school yet. I want to see this place, I haven't seen anything except the inside of our room, and the inside of chapel. I don't feel like seeing the inside of a classroom. Not now. Not yet."

"What do you want to see?"

He had started to turn around so that his back was to me. "Let's go to the gym," he said shortly.

The gym was at the other end of the school, a quarter of a mile away at least, separated from us by a field of ice. We set off without saying anything else.

By the time we had reached it sweat was running like oil from Finny's face, and when he paused involuntary tremors shook his hands and arms. The leg in its cast was like a sea anchor dragged behind. The illusion of strength I had seen in our room that morning must have been the same illusion he had used at home to deceive his doctor and his family into sending him back to Devon.

We stood on the ice-coated lawn in front of the gym while he got ready to enter it, resting himself so that he could go in with a show of energy. Later this became his habit; I often caught up with him standing in front of a building pretending to be thinking or examining the sky or taking off gloves, but it was never a convincing show. Phineas was a poor deceiver, having had no practice.

We went into the gym, along a marble hallway, and to my surprise we went on past the Trophy Room, where his name was already inscribed on one cup, one banner, and one embalmed football. I was sure that this was his goal, to mull over these lost glories. I had prepared myself for that, and even thought of several positive, uplifting aphorisms to cheer him up. But he went by it without a thought, down a stairway, steep and marble, and into the locker room. I went along mystified beside him. There was a pile of dirty towels in a corner. Finny shoved them with a crutch. "What is all this crap," he muttered with a little smile, "about no maids?"

The locker room was empty at this hour, row after row of dull green lockers separated by wide wooden benches. The ceiling was hung with pipes. It was a drab room for Devon, dull green and brown and gray, but at the far end there was a big marble archway, glisteningly white, which led to the pool.

Finny sat down on a bench, struggled out of his sheep-lined winter coat, and took a deep breath of gymnasium air. No locker room could have more pungent air than Devon's; sweat predominated, but it was richly mingled with smells of paraffin and singed rubber, of soaked wool and liniment, and for those who could interpret it, of exhaustion, lost hope and triumph and bodies battling against each other. I thought it anything but a bad smell. It was preeminently the smell of the human body after it had been used to the limit, such a smell as has meaning and poignance for any athlete, just as it has for any lover.

Phineas looked down here and there, at the exercise bar over a sand pit next to the wall, at a set of weights on the floor, at the rolled-up wrestling mat, at a pair of spiked shoes kicked under a locker.

"Same old place, isn't it?" he said, turning to me and nodding slightly.

After a moment I answered in a quiet voice, "Not exactly."

He made no pretense of not understanding me. After a pause he said, "You're going to be the big star now," in an optimistic tone, and then added with some embarrassment, "You can fill any gaps or anything." He slapped me on the back, "Get over there and chin yourself a few dozen times. What did you finally go out for anyway?"

"I finally didn't go out."

"You aren't," his eyes burned at me from his grimacing face, "still the assistant senior crew manager!"

"No, I quit that. I've just been going to gym classes. The ones they have for guys who aren't going out for anything."

He wrenched himself around on the bench. Joking was past; his mouth widened irritably. "What in hell," his voice bounded on the word in a sudden rich descent, "did you do that for?"

"It was too late to sign up for anything else," and seeing the energy to blast this excuse rushing to his face and neck I stumbled on, "and anyway with the war on there won't be many trips for the teams. I don't know, sports don't seem so important with the war on."

"Have you swallowed all that war stuff?"

"No, of course I—" I was so committed to refuting him that I had half-denied the charge before I understood it; now my eyes swung back to his face. "All what war stuff?"

"All that stuff about there being a war."

"I don't think I get what you mean."

"Do you really think that the United States of Amer-

ica is in a state of war with Nazi Germany and Impe-
rial Japan?"

"Do I really think . . ." My voice trailed off.

He stood up, his weight on the good leg, the other
resting lightly on the floor in front of him. "Don't be
a sap," he gazed with cool self-possession at me, "there
isn't any war."

"I know why you're talking like this," I said, struggling to keep up with him. "Now I understand. You're
still under the influence of some medicinal drug."

"No, you are. Everybody is." He pivoted so that he
was facing directly at me. "That's what this whole
war story is. A medicinal drug. Listen, did you ever
hear of the 'Roaring Twenties'?" I nodded very slowly
and cautiously. "When they all drank bathtub gin and
everybody who was young did just what they wanted?"

"Yes."

"Well what happened was that they didn't like that,
the preachers and the old ladies and all the stuffed
shirts. So then they tried Prohibition and everybody
just got drunker, so then they really got desperate and
arranged the Depression. That kept the people who
were young in the thirties in their places. But they
couldn't use that trick forever, so for us in the forties
they've cooked up this war fake."

"Who are 'they,' anyway?"

"The fat old men who don't want us crowding them
out of their jobs. They've made it all up. There isn't
any real food shortage, for instance. The men have all
the best steaks delivered to their clubs now. You've
noticed how they've been getting fatter lately, haven't
you?"

His tone took it thoroughly for granted that I had.
For a moment I was almost taken in by it. Then my
eyes fell on the bound and cast white mass pointing

at me, and as it was always to do, it brought me down out of Finny's world of invention, down again as I had fallen after awakening that morning, down to reality, to the facts.

"Phineas, this is all pretty amusing and everything, but I hope you don't play this game too much with yourself. You might start to believe it and then I'd have to make a reservation for you at the Funny Farm."

"In a way," deep in argument, his eyes never wavered from mine, "the whole world is on a Funny Farm now. But it's only the fat old men who get the joke."

"And you."

"Yes, and me."

"What makes you so special? Why should you get it and all the rest of us be in the dark?"

The momentum of the argument abruptly broke from his control. His face froze. "Because I've suffered," he burst out.

We drew back in amazement from this. In the silence all the flighty spirits of the morning ended between us. He sat down and turned his flushed face away from me. I sat next to him without moving for as long as my beating nerves would permit, and then I stood up and walked slowly toward anything which presented itself. It turned out to be the exercise bar. I sprang up, grabbed it, and then, in a fumbling and perhaps grotesque offering to Phineas, I chinned myself. I couldn't think of anything else, not the right words, not the right gesture. I did what I could think of.

"Do thirty of them," he mumbled in a bored voice.

I had never done ten of them. At the twelfth I discovered that he had been counting to himself because he began to count aloud in a noncommittal, half-heard voice. At eighteen there was a certain enlargement in his tone, and at twenty-three the last edges of boredom left it; he stood up, and the urgency with which he brought out the next numbers was like an invisible boost lifting me the distance of my arms, until he sang out "thirty!" with a flare of pleasure.

The moment was past. Phineas I know had been even more startled than I to discover this bitterness in himself. Neither of us ever mentioned it again, and neither of us ever forgot that it was there.

He sat down and studied his clenched hands. "Did I ever tell you," he began in a husky tone, "that I used to be aiming for the Olympics?" He wouldn't have mentioned it except that after what he had said he had to say something very personal, something deeply held. To do otherwise, to begin joking, would have been a hypocritical denial of what had happened, and Phineas was not capable of that.

I was still hanging from the bar; my hands felt as though they had sunk into it. "No, you never told me that," I mumbled into my arm.

"Well I was. And now I'm not sure, not a hundred per cent sure I'll be completely, you know, in shape by 1944. So I'm going to coach you for them instead."

"But there isn't going to be any Olympics in '44. That's only a couple of years away. The war—"

"Leave your fantasy life out of this. We're grooming you for the Olympics, pal, in 1944."

And not believing him, not forgetting that troops were being shuttled toward battlefields all over the world, I went along, as I always did, with any new invention of Finny's. There was no harm in taking aim, even if the target was a dream.

But since we were so far out of the line of fire, the chief sustenance for any sense of the war was mental.

We saw nothing real of it; all our impressions of the war were in the false medium of two dimensions—photographs in the papers and magazines, newsreels, posters—or artificially conveyed to us by a voice on the radio, or headlines across the top of a newspaper. I found that only through a continuous use of the imagination could I hold out against Finny's driving offensive in favor of peace.

And now when we were served chicken livers for dinner I couldn't help conceiving a mental picture of President Roosevelt and my father and Finny's father and numbers of other large old men sitting down to porterhouse steak in some elaborate but secluded men's secret society room. When a letter from home told me that a trip to visit relatives had been canceled because of gas rationing it was easy to visualize my father smiling silently with knowing eyes—at least as easy as it was to imagine an American force crawling through the jungles of a place called Guadalcanal—"Wherever that is," as Phineas said.

And when in chapel day after day we were exhorted to new levels of self-deprivation and hard work, with the war as their justification, it was impossible not to see that the faculty were using this excuse to drive us as they had always wanted to drive us, regardless of any war or peace.

What a joke if Finny was right after all!

But of course I didn't believe him. I was too well protected against the great fear of boys' school life, which is to be "taken in." Along with everyone else except a few professional gulls such as Leper, I rejected anything which had the smallest possibility of doubt about it. So of course I didn't believe him. But one day after our chaplain, Mr. Carhart, had become very moved by his own sermon in chapel about God in the

Foxholes, I came away thinking that if Finny's opinion of the war was unreal, Mr. Carhart's was at least as unreal. But of course I didn't believe him.

And anyway I was too occupied to think about it all. In addition to my own work, I was dividing my time between tutoring Finny in studies and being tutored by him in sports. Since so much of learning anything depends on the atmosphere in which it is taught, Finny and I, to our joint double amazement, began to make flashing progress where we had been bumblers before.

Mornings we got up at six to run. I dressed in a gym sweat suit with a towel tucked around my throat, and Finny in pajamas, ski boots and his sheep-lined coat.

A morning shortly before Christmas vacation brought my reward. I was to run the course Finny had laid out, four times around an oval walk which circled the Headmaster's home, a large rambling, doubtfully Colonial white mansion. Next to the house there was a patriarchal elm tree, against the trunk of which Finny leaned and shouted at me as I ran a large circle around him.

This plain of snow shone a powdery white that morning; the sun blazed icily somewhere too low on the horizon to be seen directly, but its clean rays shed a blue-white glimmer all around us. The northern sunshine seemed to pick up faint particles of whiteness floating in the air and powdering the sleek blue sky. Nothing stirred. The bare arching branches of the elm seemed laid into this motionless sky. As I ran the sound of my footfalls was pitched off short in the vast immobile dawn, as though there was no room amid so many glittering sights for any sound to intrude. The figure of Phineas was set against the bulk of the tree; he shouted now and then, but these sounds too were quickly absorbed and dispelled.

And he needed to give no advice that morning. After making two circuits of the walk every trace of energy was as usual completely used up, and as I drove myself on all my scattered aches found their usual way to a profound seat of pain in my side. My lungs as usual were fed up with all this work, and from now on would only go rackingly through the motions. My knees were boneless again, ready any minute to let my lower legs telescope up into the thighs. My head felt as though different sections of the cranium were grinding into each other.

Then, for no reason at all, I felt magnificent. It was as though my body until that instant had simply been lazy, as though the aches and exhaustion were all imagined, created from nothing in order to keep me from truly exerting myself. Now my body seemed at last to say, "Well, if you must have it, here!" and an accession of strength came flooding through me. Buoyed up, I forgot my usual feeling of routine self-pity when working out, I lost myself, oppressed mind along with aching body; all entanglements were shed, I broke into the clear.

After the fourth circuit, like sitting in a chair, I pulled up in front of Phineas.

"You're not even winded," he said.

"I know."

"You found your rhythm, didn't you, that third time around. Just as you came into that straight part there."

"Yes, right there."

"You've been pretty lazy all along, haven't you?"

"Yes, I guess I have been."

"You didn't even know anything about yourself."

"I don't guess I did, in a way."

"Well," he gathered the sheepskin collar around his throat, "now you know. And stop talking like a Georgia cracker—'don't guess I did'!" Despite this gibe he was rather impersonal toward me. He seemed older that morning, and leaning quietly against that great tree wrapped in his heavy coat, he seemed smaller too. Or perhaps it was only that I, inside the same body, had felt myself all at once grown bigger.

We proceeded slowly back to the dormitory. On the steps going in we met Mr. Ludsbury coming out.

"I've been watching you from my window," he said in his hooting voice with a rare trace of personal interest. "What are you up to, Forrester, training for the Commandos?" There was no rule explicitly forbidding exercise at such an hour, but it was not expected; ordinarily therefore Mr. Ludsbury would have disapproved. But the war had modified even his standards; all forms of physical exercise had become conventional for the Duration.

I mumbled some abashed answer, but it was Phineas who made the clear response.

"He's developing into a real athlete," he said matter-of-factly. "We're aiming for the '44 Olympics."

Mr. Ludsbury emitted a single chuckle from deep in his throat, then his face turned brick red momentarily and he assumed his customary sententiousness. "Games are all right in their place," he said, "and I won't bore you with the Eton Playing Fields observation, but all exercise today is aimed of course at the approaching Waterloo. Keep that in your sights at all times, won't you."

Finny's face set in determination, with the older look I had just detected in him. "No," he said.

I don't believe any student had ever said "No" flatly to Mr. Ludsbury before. It flustered him uncontrollably. His face turned brick red again, and for a moment I thought he was going to run away. Then he said something so rapid, throaty, and clipped that neither of us understood it, turned quickly and strode off across the quadrangle.

"He's really sincere, he thinks there's a war on," said Finny in simple wonder. "Now why wouldn't he know?" He pondered Mr. Ludsbury's exclusion from the plot of the fat old men as we watched his figure, reedy even in his winter wraps, move away from us. Then the light broke. "Oh, of course!" he cried. "Too thin. Of course."

I stood there pitying Mr. Ludsbury for his fatal thinness and reflecting that after all he had always had a gullible side.

9

This was my first but not my last lapse into Finny's vision of peace. For hours, and sometimes for days, I fell without realizing it into the private explanation of the world. Not that I ever believed that the whole production of World War II was a trick of the eye manipulated by a bunch of calculating fat old men, appealing though this idea was. What deceived me was my own happiness; for peace is indivisible, and the surrounding world confusion found no reflection inside me. So I ceased to have any real sense of it.

This was not shaken even by the enlistment of Leper Lepellier. In fact that made the war seem more unreal than ever. No real war could draw Leper voluntarily away from his snails and beaver dams. His enlistment seemed just another of Leper's vagaries, such as the time he slept on top of Mount Katahdin in Maine where each morning the sun first strikes United States territory. On that morning, satisfying one of his urges to participate in nature, Leper Lepellier was the first thing the rising sun struck in the United States.

Early in January, when we had all just returned from the Christmas holidays, a recruiter from the United States ski troops showed a film to the senior class in the Renaissance Room. To Leper it revealed what all of

us were seeking: a recognizable and friendly face to
the war. Skiers in white shrouds winged down virgin
slopes, silent as angels, and then, realistically, herringboned up again, but herringboned in cheerful, sunburned bands, with clear eyes and white teeth and
chests full of vigor-laden mountain air. It was the
cleanest image of war I had ever seen; even the Air
Force, reputedly so high above the infantry's mud, was
stained with axle grease by comparison, and the Navy
was vulnerable to scurvy. Nothing tainted these white
warriors of winter as they swooped down their spotless
mountainsides, and this cool, clean response to war
glided straight into Leper's Vermont heart.

"How do you like that!" he whispered to me in a
wondering voice during these scenes. "How do you like
that!"

"You know, I think these are pictures of Finnish ski
troops," Phineas whispered on the other side, "and I
want to know when they start shooting our allies the
Bolsheviks. Unless that war between them was a fake
too, which I'm pretty sure it was."

After the movie ended and the lights came on to
illuminate the murals of Tuscany and the painted clas-
sical galleries around us, Leper still sat amazed in his
folding chair. Ordinarily he talked little, and the number of words which came from him now indicated that
this was a turning point in his life.

"You know what? Now I see what racing skiing is all
about. It's all right to miss seeing the trees and the
countryside and all the other things when you've got to
be in a hurry. And when you're in a War you've got to
be in a hurry. Don't you? So I guess maybe racing
skiers weren't ruining the sport after all. They were
preparing it, if you see what I mean, for the future.

Everything has to evolve or else it perishes." Finny and I had stood up, and Leper looked earnestly from one to the other of us from his chair. "Take the house-fly. If it hadn't developed all those split-second reflexes it would have become extinct long ago."

"You mean it adapted itself to the fly swatter?" queried Phineas.

"That's right. And skiing had to learn to move just as fast or it would have been wiped out by this war. Yes, sir. You know what? I'm almost glad this war came along. It's like a test, isn't it, and only the things and the people who've been evolving the right way sur-vive."

You usually listened to Leper's quiet talking with half a mind, but this theory of his brought me to close attention. How did it apply to me, and to Phineas? How, most of all, did it apply to Leper?

"I'm going to enlist in these ski troops," he went on mildly, so unemphatically that my mind went back to half-listening. Threats to enlist that winter were always declaimed like Brinker's, with a grinding of back teeth and a flashing of eyes; I had already heard plenty of them. But only Leper's was serious.

A week later he was gone. He had been within a few weeks of his eighteenth birthday, and with it all chance of enlistment, of choosing a service rather than being drafted into one, would have disappeared. The ski movie had decided him. "I always thought the war would come for me when it wanted me," he said when he came to say goodbye the last day. "I never thought I'd be going to it. I'm really glad I saw that movie in time, you bet I am." Then, as the Devon School's first recruit to World War II, he went out my doorway with his white stocking cap bobbing behind.

It probably would have been better for all of us if someone like Brinker had been the first to go. He could have been depended upon to take a loud dramatic departure, so that the school would have reverberated for weeks afterward with Brinker's Last Words, Brinker's Military Bearing, Brinker's Sense of Duty. And all of us, influenced by the vacuum of his absence, would have felt the touch of war as a daily fact.

But the disappearing tail of Leper's cap inspired none of this. For a few days the war was more unimaginable than ever. We didn't mention it and we didn't mention Leper, until at last Brinker found a workable point of view. One day in the Butt Room he read aloud a rumor in a newspaper about an attempt on Hitler's life. He lowered the paper, gazed in a visionary way in front of him, and then remarked, "That was Leper, of course."

This established our liaison with World War II. The Tunisian campaign became "Leper's liberation"; the bombing of the Ruhr was greeted by Brinker with hurt surprise: "He didn't tell us he'd left the ski troops"; the torpedoing of the *Scharnhorst:* "At it again." Leper sprang up all over the world at the core of every Allied success. We talked about Leper's stand at Stalingrad, Leper on the Burma Road, Leper's convoy to Archangel; we surmised that the crisis over the leadership of the Free French would be resolved by the appointment of neither de Gaulle nor Giraud but Lepellier; we knew, better than the newspapers, that it was not the Big Three but the Big Four who were running the war.

In the silences between jokes about Leper's glories we wondered whether we ourselves would measure up to the humblest minimum standard of the army. I did not know everything there was to know about myself, and knew that I did not know it; I wondered in the silences between jokes about Leper whether the still hidden parts of myself might contain the Sad Sack, the outcast, or the coward. We were all at our funniest about Leper, and we all secretly hoped that Leper, that incompetent, was as heroic as we said.

Everyone contributed to this legend except Phineas. At the outset, with the attempt on Hitler's life, Finny had said, "If someone gave Leper a loaded gun and put it at Hitler's temple, he'd miss." There was a general shout of outrage, and then we recommended the building of Leper's triumphal arch around Brinker's keystone. Phineas took no part in it, and since little else was talked about in the Butt Room he soon stopped going there and stopped me from going as well—"How do you expect to be an athlete if you smoke like a forest fire?" He drew me increasingly away from the Butt Room crowd, away from Brinker and Chet and all other friends, into a world inhabited by just himself and me, where there was no war at all, just Phineas and me alone among all the people of the world, training for the Olympics of 1944.

Saturday afternoons are terrible in a boys' school, especially in the winter. There is no football game; it is not possible, as it is in the spring, to take bicycle trips into the surrounding country. Not even the most grinding student can feel required to lose himself in his books, since there is Sunday ahead, long, lazy, quiet Sunday, to do any homework.

And these Saturdays are worst in the late winter when the snow has lost its novelty and its shine, and the school seems to have been reduced to only a network of drains. During the brief thaw in the early afternoon there is a dismal gurgling of dirty water seeping down pipes and along gutters, a gray seamy shifting beneath the crust of snow, which cracks to show patches of frozen mud beneath. Shrubbery loses its bright snow headgear and stands bare and frail, too undernourished to hide the drains it was intended to hide. These are the days when going into any building you cross a mat of dirt and cinders led in by others before you, thinning and finally trailing off in the corridors. The sky is an empty hopeless gray and gives the impression that this is its eternal shade. Winter's occupation seems to have conquered, overrun and destroyed everything, so that now there is no longer any resistance movement left in nature; all the juices are dead, every sprig of vitality snapped, and now winter itself, an old, corrupt, tired conqueror, loosens its grip on the desolation, recedes a little, grows careless in its watch; sick of victory and enfeebled by the absence of challenge, it begins itself to withdraw from the ruined countryside. The drains alone are active, and on these Saturdays their noises sound a dull recessional to winter.

Only Phineas failed to see what was so depressing. Just as there was no war in his philosophy, there was also no dreary weather. As I have said, all weathers delighted Phineas. "You know what we'd better do next Saturday?" he began in one of his voices, the low-pitched and evenly melodic one which for some reason always reminded me of a Rolls-Royce moving along a highway. "We'd better organize the Winter Carnival."

We were sitting in our room, on either side of the single large window framing a square of featureless gray sky. Phineas was resting his cast, which was a considerably smaller one now, on the desk and thoughtfully pressing designs into it with a pocket knife. "What Winter Carnival?" I asked.

"*The* Winter Carnival. The Devon Winter Carnival."

"There isn't any Devon Winter Carnival and never has been."

"There is now. We'll have it in that park next to the Naguamsett. The main attraction will be sports, naturally, featuring I expect a ski jump—"

"A ski jump! That park's as flat as a pancake."

"—and some slalom races, and I think a little track. But we've got to have some snow statues too, and a little music, and something to eat. Now, which committee do you want to head?"

I gave him a wintry smile. "The snow statues committee."

"I knew you would. You always were secretly arty, weren't you? I'll organize the sports, Brinker can handle the music and food, and then we need somebody to kind of beautify the place, a few holly wreaths and things like that. Someone good with plants and shrubbery. I know. Leper."

From looking at the star he was imprinting in his cast I looked quickly up at his face. "Leper's gone."

"Oh yeah, so he is. Leper *would* be gone. Well, somebody else then."

And because it was Finny's idea, it happened as he said, although not as easily as some of his earlier inspirations. For our dormitory was less enthusiastic about almost everything with each succeeding week. Brinker for example had begun a long, decisive sequence of withdrawals from school activity ever since the morning I deserted his enlistment plan. He had not resented my change of heart, and in fact had immediately undergone one himself. If he could not enlist—and for all his self-sufficiency Brinker could not do much without company—he could at least cease to be so multifariously civilian. So he resigned the presidency of the Golden Fleece Debating Society, stopped writing his school spirit column for the newspaper, dropped the chairmanship of the Underprivileged Local Children subcommittee of the Good Samaritan Confraternity, stilled his baritone in the chapel choir, and even, in his most impressive burst of irresponsibility, resigned from the Student Advisory Committee to the Headmaster's Discretionary Benevolent Fund. His well-bred clothes had disappeared; these days he wore khaki pants supported by a garrison belt, and boots which rattled when he walked.

"Who wants a Winter Carnival?" he said in the disillusioned way he had lately developed when I brought it up. "What are we supposed to be celebrating?"

"Winter, I guess."

"Winter!" He gazed out of his window at the vacant sky and seeping ground. "Frankly, I just don't see anything to celebrate, winter or spring or anything else."

"This is the first time Finny's gotten going on anything since . . . he came back."

"He has been kind of nonfunctional, hasn't he? He isn't *brooding*, is he?"

"No, he wouldn't brood."

"No, I don't suppose he would. Well, if you think it's something Finny really wants. Still, there's never been a Winter Carnival here. I think there's probably a rule against it."

"I see," I said in a tone which made Brinker raise his eyes and lock them with mine. In that plotters' glance all his doubts vanished, for Brinker the Lawgiver had turned rebel for the Duration.

The Saturday was battleship gray. Throughout the morning equipment for the Winter Carnival had been spirited out of the dormitory and down to the small in-

complete public park on the bank of the Naguamsett
River. Brinker supervised the transfer, rattling up and
down the stairwell and giving orders. He made me
think of a pirate captain disposing of the booty. Several jugs of very hard cider which he had browbeaten
away from some lowerclassmen were the most cautiously guarded treasure. They were buried in the
snow near a clump of evergreens in the center of the
park, and Brinker stationed his roommate, Brownie
Perkins, to guard them with his life. He meant this literally, and Brownie knew it. So he trembled alone
there in the middle of the park for hours, wondering
what would happen if he had an attack of appendicitis,
unnerved by the thoughts of a fainting spell, horrified
by the realization that he might have to move his
bowels, until at last we came. Then Brownie crept back
to the dormitory, too exhausted to enjoy the carnival
at all. On this day of high illegal competitiveness, no
one noticed.

The buried cider was half-consciously plotted at the
hub of the carnival. Around it sprang up large, sloppy
statues, easily modeled because of the snow's damp-
ness. Nearby, entirely out of place in this snowscape,
like a dowager in a saloon, there was a heavy circular
classroom table, carried there by superhuman exertions
the night before on Finny's insistence that he had to
have *something* to display the prizes on. On it rested
the prizes—Finny's icebox, hidden all these months in
the dormitory basement, a Webster's Collegiate Dic-
tionary with all the most stimulating words marked, a
set of York barbells, the *Iliad* with the English translation of each sentence written above it, Brinker's file of
Betty Grable photographs, a lock of hair cut under
duress from the head of Hazel Brewster, the professional town belle, a handwoven rope ladder with the

proviso that it should be awarded to someone occupying a room on the third floor or higher, a forged draft registration card, and $4.13 from the Headmaster's Discretionary Benevolent Fund. Brinker placed this last prize on the table with such silent dignity that we all thought it was better not to ask any questions about it.

Phineas sat behind the table in a heavily carved black walnut chair; the arms ended in two lions' heads, and the legs ended in paws gripping wheels now sunk in the snow. He had made the purchase that morning. Phineas bought things only on impulse and only when he had the money, and since the two states rarely coincided his purchases were few and strange.

Chet Douglass stood next to him holding his trumpet. Finny had regretfully given up the plan of inviting the school band to supply music, since it would have spread news of our carnival to every corner of the campus. Chet in any case was an improvement over that cacophony. He was a slim, fair-skinned boy with a ball of curly auburn hair curving over his forehead, and he devoted himself to playing two things, tennis and the trumpet. He did both with such easy, inborn skill that after observing him I had begun to think that I could master either one any weekend I tried. Much like the rest of us on the surface, he had an underlying obliging and considerate strain which barred him from being a really important member of the class. You had to be rude at least sometimes and edgy often to be credited with "personality," and without that accolade no one at Devon could be anyone. No one, with the exception of course of Phineas.

To the left of the Prize Table Brinker straddled his cache of cider; behind him was the clump of evergreens, and behind them there was after all a gentle rise, where the Ski Jump Committee was pounding snow into a little take-off ramp whose lip was perhaps a foot higher than the slope of the rise. From there our line of snow statues, unrecognizable artistic attacks on the Headmaster, Mr. Ludsbury, Mr. Patch-Withers, Dr. Stanpole, the new dietitian, and Hazel Brewster curved in an enclosing half-circle to the icy, muddy, lisping edge of the tidewater Naguamsett and back to the other side of the Prize Table.

When the ski jump was ready there was a certain amount of milling around; twenty boys, tightly reined in all winter, stood now as though with the bit firmly clamped between their teeth, ready to stampede. Phineas should have started the sports events but he was absorbed in cataloguing the prizes. All eyes swung next upon Brinker. He had been holding a pose above his cider of Gibraltar invulnerability; he continued to gaze challengingly around him until he began to realize that wherever he looked, calculating eyes looked back.

"All right, all right," he said roughly, "let's get started."

The ragged circle around him moved perceptibly closer.

"Let's get going," he yelled. "Come on, Finny. What's first?"

Phineas had one of those minds which could record what is happening in the background and do nothing about it because something else was preoccupying him. He seemed to sink deeper into his list.

"Phineas!" Brinker pronounced his name with a maximum use of the teeth. "What is next?"

Still the sleek brown head bent mesmerized over the list.

"What's the big hurry, Brinker?" someone from the

tightening circle asked with dangerous gentleness. "What's the big rush?"

"We can't stand here all day," he blurted. "We've got to get started if we're going to have this damn thing. What's *next*? Phineas!"

At last the recording in Finny's mind reached its climax. He looked vaguely up, studied the straddling, at-bay figure of Brinker at the core of the poised perimeter of boys, hesitated, blinked, and then in his organ voice said good-naturedly, "Next? Well that's pretty clear. You are."

Chet released from his trumpet the opening, lifting, barbaric call of a bullfight, and the circle of boys broke wildly over Brinker. He flailed back against the evergreens, and the jugs appeared to spring out of the snow. "What the hell," he kept yelling, off balance among the branches. "*What . . . the . . . hell!*" By then his cider, which he had apparently expected to dole out according to his own governing whim, was disappearing. There was going to be no government, even by whim, even by Brinker's whim, on this Saturday at Devon.

From a scramble of contenders I got one of the jugs, elbowed off a counterattack, opened it, sampled it, choked, and then went through with my original plan by stopping Brinker's mouth with it. His eyes bulged, and blood vessels in his throat began to pulsate, until at length I lowered the jug.

He gave me a long, pondering look, his face closed and concentrating while behind it his mind plainly teetered between fury and hilarity; I think if I had batted an eye he would have hit me. The carnival's breaking apart into a riot hung like a bomb between us. I kept on looking expressionlessly back at him until beneath a blackening scowl his mouth opened enough to fire out the words, "I've been violated."

I jerked the jug to my mouth and took a huge gulp of cider in relief, and the violence latent in the day drifted away; perhaps the Naguamsett carried it out on the receding tide. Brinker strode through the swirl of boys to Phineas. "I formally declare," he bellowed, "that these Games are open."

"You can't do that," Finny said rebukingly. "Who ever heard of opening the Games without the sacred fire from Olympus?"

Sensing that I must act as the Chorus, I registered on my face the universally unheard-of quality of the Games without fire. "Fire, fire," I said across the damp snow.

"We'll sacrifice one of the prizes," said Phineas, seizing the *Iliad*. He sprinkled the pages with cider to make them more inflammable, touched a match to them, and a little jet of flame curled upward. The Games, alight with Homer and cider, were open.

Chet Douglass, leaning against the side of the Prize Table, continued to blow musical figures for his own enlightenment. Forgetful of us and the athletic programing Finny now put into motion, he strolled here and there, sometimes at the start of the ski jump competition, blowing an appropriate call, more often invoking the serene order of Haydn, or a high, remote, arrogant Spanish world, or the cheerful, lowdown carelessness of New Orleans.

The hard cider began to take charge of us. Or I wonder now whether it wasn't cider but our own exuberance which intoxicated us, sent restraint flying, causing Brinker to throw the football block on the statue of the Headmaster, giving me, as I put on the skis and slid down the small slope and off the miniature ski jump a sensation of soaring flight, of hurtling high and far through space; inspiring Phineas, during one of Chet's Spanish inventions, to climb onto the Prize Table and with only one leg to create a droll dance among the prizes, springing and spinning from one bare space to another, cleanly missing Hazel Brewster's hair, never marring by a misstep the pictures of Betty Grable. Under the influence not I know of the hardest cider but of his own inner joy at life for a moment as it should be, as it was meant to be in his nature, Phineas recaptured that magic gift for existing primarily in space, one foot conceding briefly to gravity its rights before spinning him off again into the air. It was his wildest demonstration of himself, of himself in the kind of world he loved; it was his choreography of peace.

And when he stopped and sat down among the prizes and said, "Now we're going to have the Decathlon. Quiet everybody, our Olympic candidate Gene Forrester, is now going to qualify," it wasn't cider which made me in this moment champion of everything he ordered, to run as though I were the abstraction of speed, to walk the half-circle of statues on my hands, to balance on my head on top of the icebox on top of the Prize Table, to jump if he had asked it across the Naguamsett and land crashing in the middle of Quackenbush's boathouse, to accept at the end of it amid a clatter of applause—for on this day even the schoolboy egotism of Devon was conjured away—a wreath made from the evergreen trees which Phineas placed on my head. It wasn't the cider which made me surpass myself, it was this liberation we had torn from the gray encroachments of 1943, the escape we had concocted, this afternoon of momentary, illusory, special and separate peace.

And it was this which caused me not to notice Brownie Perkins rejoin us from the dormitory, and not to hear what he was saying until Finny cried hilariously, "A telegram for Gene? It's the Olympic Committee. They want you! Of course they want you! Give it to me, Brownie, I'll read it aloud to this assembled host." And it was this which drained away as I watched Finny's face pass through all the gradations between uproariousness and shock.

I took the telegram from Phineas, facing in advance whatever the destruction was. That was what I learned to do that winter.

I HAVE ESCAPED AND NEED HELP. I AM AT CHRISTMAS LOCATION. YOU UNDERSTAND. NO NEED TO RISK ADDRESS HERE. MY SAFETY DEPENDS ON YOU COMING AT ONCE.

(signed) YOUR BEST FRIEND,

ELWIN LEPER LEPELLIER.

10

That night I made for the first time the kind of journey which later became the monotonous routine of my life: traveling through an unknown countryside from one unknown settlement to another. The next year this became the dominant activity, or rather passivity, of my army career, not fighting, not marching, but this kind of nighttime ricochet; for as it turned out I never got to the war.

I went into uniform at the time when our enemies began to recede so fast that there had to be a hurried telescoping of military training plans. Programs scheduled to culminate in two years became outmoded in six months, and crowds of men gathered for them in one place were dispersed to twenty others. A new weapon appeared and those of us who had traveled to three or four bases mastering the old one were sent on to a fifth, sixth, and seventh to master the new. The closer victory came the faster we were shuttled around America in pursuit of a role to play in a drama which suddenly, underpopulated from the first, now had too many actors. Or so it seemed. In reality there would have been, as always, too few, except that the last act, a mass assault against suicidally-defended Japan, never took place. I and my year—not "my generation" for destiny now cut too finely for that old phrase—I and those of my year were preeminently eligible for that. Most of us, so it was estimated, would be killed. But the men a little bit older closed in on the enemy faster than predicted, and then there was the final holocaust of the Bomb. It seemed to have saved our lives.

So journeys through unknown parts of America became my chief war memory, and I think of the first of them as this nighttime trip to Leper's. There was no question of where to find him; "I am at Christmas location" meant that he was at home. He lived far up in Vermont, where at this season of the year even the paved main highways are bumpy and buckling from the freezing weather, and each house executes a lonely holding action against the cold. The natural state of things is coldness, and houses are fragile havens, holdouts in a death landscape, unforgettably comfortable, simple though they are, just because of their warmth.

Leper's was one of these hearths perched by itself on a frozen hillside. I reached it in the early morning after this night which presaged my war; a bleak, draughty train ride, a damp depot seemingly near no town whatever, a bus station in which none of the people were fully awake, or seemed clean, or looked as though they had homes anywhere; a bus which passengers entered and left at desolate stopping places in the blackness; a chilled nighttime wandering in which I tried to decipher between lapses into stale sleep, the meaning of Leper's telegram.

I reached the town at dawn, and encouraged by the returning light, and coffee in a thick white cup, I accepted a hopeful interpretation. Leper had "escaped." You didn't "escape" from the army, so he must have escaped from something else. The most logical thing a soldier escapes from is danger, death, the enemy. Since Leper hadn't been overseas the enemy must have been in this country. And the only enemies in this country would be spies. Leper had escaped from spies.

I seized this conclusion and didn't try to go beyond it. I suppose all our Butt Room stories about him intriguing around the world had made me half-ready to half-believe something like this. I felt a measureless relief when it occurred to me. There was some color, some hope, some life in this war after all. The first friend of mine who ever went into it tangled almost immediately with spies. I began to hope that after all this wasn't going to be such a bad war.

The Lepellier house was not far out of town, I was told. There was no taxi, I was also told, and there was no one, I did not need to be told, who would offer to drive me out there. This was Vermont. But if that meant austerity toward strangers it also meant mornings of glory such as this one, in which the snow, white almost to blueness, lay like a soft comforter over the hills, and birches and pines indestructibly held their ground, rigid lines against the snow and sky, very thin and very strong like Vermonters.

The sun was the blessing of the morning, the one celebrating element, an aesthete with no purpose except to shed radiance. Everything else was sharp and hard, but this Grecian sun evoked joy from every angularity and blurred with brightness the stiff face of the countryside. As I walked briskly out the road the wind knifed at my face, but this sun caressed the back of my neck.

The road led out along the side of a ridge, and after a mile or so I saw the house that must be Leper's, riding the top of the slope. It was another brittle-looking Vermont house, white of course, with long and narrow windows like New England faces. Behind one of them hung a gold star which announced that a son of the house was serving the country, and behind another stood Leper.

Although I was walking straight toward his front door he beckoned me on several times, and he never took his eyes from me, as though it was they which held me to my course. He was still at this ground-floor window when I reached the door and so I opened it myself and stepped into the hallway. Leper had come to the entrance of the room on the right, the dining room.

"Come in here," he said, "I spend most of my time in here."

As usual there were no preliminaries. "What do you do that for, Leper? It's not very comfortable, is it?"

"Well, it's a useful room."

"Yes, I guess it's useful, all right."

"You aren't lost for something to do in dining rooms. It's in the living room where people can't figure out what to do with themselves. People get problems in living rooms."

"Bedrooms too." It was a try toward relieving the foreboding in his manner; it only worked to deepen it.

He turned away, and I followed him into an under-furnished dining room of high-backed chairs, rugless floor, and cold fireplace. "If you want to be in a really functional room," I began with false heartiness, "you ought to spend your time in the bathroom then."

He looked at me, and I noticed the left side of his upper lip lift once or twice as though he was about to snarl or cry. Then I realized that this had nothing to do with his mood, that it was involuntary.

He sat down at the head of the table in the only chair with arms, his father's chair I supposed. I took

off my coat and sat in a place at the middle of the
table, with my back to the fireplace. There at least I
could look at the sun rejoicing on the snow.

"In here you never wonder what's going to happen.
You know the meals will come in three times a day for
instance."

"I'll bet your mother isn't too pleased when she's trying to get one ready."

Force sprang into his expression for the first time.
"What's she got to be pleased about!" He glared challengingly into my startled face. "I'm pleasing *myself!*"
he cried fervently, and I saw tears trembling in his
eyes.

"Well, she's probably pleased." Any words would
serve, the more irrelevant and superficial the better,
any words which would stop him; I didn't want to see
this. "She's probably pleased to have you home again."

His face resumed its dull expression. The responsibility for continuing the conversation, since I had
forced it to be superficial, was mine. "How long'll you
be here?"

He shrugged, a look of disgust with my question
crossing his face. The careful politeness he had always
had was gone.

"Well, if you're on furlough you must know when
you have to be back." I said this in what I thought of
at the time as my older voice, a little businesslike and
experienced. "The army doesn't give out passes and
then say 'Come back when you've had enough, hear?' "

"I didn't get any pass," he groaned; with the sliding
despair of his face and his clenched hands, that's what
it was; a groan.

"I know you said," I spoke in short, expressionless
syllables, "that you 'escaped.' " I no longer wanted this
to be true, I no longer wanted it to be connected with

spies or desertion or anything out of the ordinary. I
knew it was going to be, and I no longer wanted it
to be.

"I *escaped!*" the word surging out in a voice and in-
tensity that was not Leper's. His face was furious, but
his eyes denied the fury; instead they saw it before
them. They were filled with terror.

"What do you mean, you escaped?" I said sharply.
"You don't escape from the army."

"That's what you say. But that's because you're talking through your hat." His eyes were furious now too,
glaring blindly at me. "What do you know about it,
anyway?" None of this could have been said by the
Leper of the beaver dam.

"Well I—how am I supposed to answer that? I know
what's normal in the army, that's all."

"Normal," he repeated bitterly. "What a stupid-ass
word that is. I suppose that's what you're thinking
about, isn't it? That's what you would be thinking
about, somebody like you. You're thinking I'm not normal, aren't you? I can see what you're thinking—I see
a lot I never saw before"—his voice fell to a querulous
whisper—"you're thinking I'm psycho."

I gathered what the word meant. I hated the sound
of it at once. It opened up a world I had not known
existed—"mad" or "crazy" or "a screw loose," those
were the familiar words. "Psycho" had a sudden men-
tal-ward reality about it, a systematic, diagnostic
sound. It was as though Leper had learned it while in
captivity, far from Devon or Vermont or any experience we had in common, as though it were in Japanese.

Fear seized my stomach like a cramp. I didn't care
what I said to him now; it was myself I was worried
about. For if Leper was psycho it was the army which
had done it to him, and I and all of us were on the

brink of the army. "You make me sick, you and your damn army words."

"They were going to give me," he was almost laughing, everywhere but in his eyes which continued to oppose all he said, "they were going to give me a discharge, a Section Eight discharge."

As a last defense I had always taken refuge in a scornful superiority, based on nothing. I sank back in the chair, eyebrows up, shoulders shrugging. "I don't even know what you're talking about. You just don't make any sense at all. It's all Japanese to me."

"A Section Eight discharge is for the nuts in the service, the psychos, the Funny Farm candidates. Now do you know what I'm talking about? They give you a Section Eight discharge, like a dishonorable discharge only worse. You can't get a job after that. Everybody wants to see your discharge, and when they see a Section Eight they look at you kind of funny—the kind of expression you've got on your face, like you were looking at someone with their nose blown off but don't want them to know you're disgusted—they look at you that way and then they say, 'Well, there doesn't seem to be an opening here at present.' You're screwed for life, that's what a Section Eight discharge means."

"You don't have to yell at me, there's nothing wrong with my hearing."

"Then that's tough shit for you, Buster. Then they've got you."

"Nobody's *got* me."

"Oh they've got you all right."

"Don't tell me who's got me and who hasn't got me. Who do you think you're talking to? Stick to your snails, Lepellier."

He began to laugh again. "You always were a lord of the manor, weren't you? A swell guy, except when the

chips were down. You always were a savage underneath. I always knew that only I never admitted it.
But in the last few weeks," despair broke into his face
again, "I admitted a hell of a lot to myself. Not about
you. Don't flatter yourself. I wasn't thinking about you.
Why the hell should I think about you? Did you ever
think about me? I thought about myself, and Ma, and
the old man, and *pleasing* them all the time. Well,
never mind about that now. It's you we happen to be
talking about now. Like a savage underneath. Like,"
now there was the blind confusion in his eyes again, a
wild slyness around his mouth, "like that time you
knocked Finny out of the tree."

I sprang out of the chair. "You stupid crazy bastard—"

Still laughing, "Like that time you crippled him for
life."

I shoved my foot against the rung of his chair and
kicked. Leper went over in his chair and collapsed
against the floor. Laughing and crying he lay with his
head on the floor and his knees up, ". . . always were a
savage underneath."

Quick heels coming down the stairs, and his mother,
large, soft, and gentle-looking, quivered at the entrance. "What on earth happened? Elwin!"

"I'm terribly—it was a mistake," I listened objec-
tively to my own voice, "he said something crazy. I
forgot myself—I forgot that he's, there's something the
matter with his nerves, isn't there? He didn't know
what he was saying."

"Well, good heaven, the boy is ill." We both moved
swiftly to help up the chuckling Leper. "Did you come
here to abuse him?"

"I'm terribly sorry," I muttered. "I'd better get going."

Mrs. Lepellier was helping Leper toward the stairs. "Don't go," he said between chuckles, "stay for lunch. You can count on it. Always three meals a day, war or peace, in this room."

And I did stay. Sometimes you are too ashamed to leave. That was true now. And sometimes you need too much to know the facts, and so humbly and stupidly you stay. That was true now too.

It was an abundant Vermont lunch, more like a dinner, and at first it had no more reality than a meal in the theater. Leper ate almost nothing, but my own appetite deepened my disgrace. I ate everything within reach, and then had to ask, face aflame with embarrassment, for more to be passed to me. But that led to this hard-to-believe transformation: Mrs. Lepellier began to be reconciled to me because I liked her cooking. Toward the end of the meal she became able to speak to me directly, in her high but gentle and modulated voice, and I was so clumsy and fumbling and embarrassed that my behavior throughout lunch amounted to one long and elaborate apology which, when she offered me a second dessert, I saw she had accepted. "He's a good boy underneath," she must have thought, "a terrible temper, no self-control, but he's sorry, and he is a good boy underneath." Leper was closer to the truth. ~~Savage underneath~~

She suggested he and I take a walk after lunch. Leper now seemed all obedience, and except for the fact that he never looked at his mother, the ideal son. So he put on some odds and ends of clothing, some canvas and woolen and flannel pulled on to form a patchwork against the cutting wind, and we trailed out the back door into the splendor of the failing sunshine. I did not have New England in my bones; I was a guest in this country, even though by now a familiar one, and I could never see a totally extinguished winter field without thinking it unnatural. I would tramp along trying to decide whether corn had grown there in the summer, or whether it had been a pasture, or what it could ever have been, and in that deep layer of the mind where all is judged by the five senses and primitive expectation, I knew that nothing would ever grow there again. We roamed across one of these wastes, our feet breaking through at each step the thin surface crust of ice into a layer of soft snow underneath, and I waited for Leper, in this wintery outdoors he loved, to come to himself again. Just as I knew the field could never grow again, I knew that Leper could not be wild or bitter or psycho tramping across the hills of Vermont.

"Is there an army camp in Vermont?" I asked, so sure in my illusion that I risked making him talk, risked even making him talk about the army.

"I don't think there is."

"There ought to be. That's where they should have sent you. Then you wouldn't have gotten nervous."

"Yeah." A half chuckle. "I was what they call 'nervous in the service.'"

Exaggerated laughter from me. "Is that what they call it?"

Leper didn't bother to make a rejoinder. Before there had always been his polite capping of remarks like this: "Yes, they do, that's what they call it"—but today he glanced speculatively at me and said nothing.

We walked on, the crust cracking uneasily under us. "Nervous in the service," I said. "That sounds like one of Brinker's poems."

"That bastard!"

"You wouldn't know Brinker these days the way he's changed—"

"I'd know that bastard if he'd changed into Snow White."

"Well. He hasn't changed into Snow White."

"That's too bad," the strained laughter was back in his voice, "Snow White with Brinker's face on her. There's a picture," then he broke into sobs.

"Leper! What is it? What's the matter, Leper? Leper!"

Hoarse, cracking sobs broke from him; another ounce of grief and he would have begun tearing his country-store clothes. "Leper! Leper!" This exposure drew us violently together; I was the closest person in the world to him now, and he to me. "Leper, for God sakes, Leper." I was about to cry myself. "Stop that, now just stop. Don't do that. Stop doing that, Leper."

When he became quieter, not less despairing but too exhausted to keep on, I said, "I'm sorry I brought up Brinker. I didn't know you hated him so much." Leper didn't look capable of such hates. Especially now, with his rapid plumes of breath puffing out as from a toiling steam engine, his nose and eyes gone red, and his cheeks red too, in large, irregular blotches —Leper had the kind of fragile fair skin given to high, unhealthy coloring. He was all color, painted at random, but none of it highlighted his grief. Instead of desperate and hate-filled, he looked, with his checkered outfit and blotchy face, like a half-prepared clown.

"I don't really hate Brinker, I don't really hate him, not any more than anybody else." His swimming eyes cautiously explored me. The wind lifted a sail of snow and billowed it past us. "It was only—" he drew in his breath so sharply that it made a whistling sound—"the idea of *his* face on a *woman's* body. That's what made me psycho. Ideas like that. I don't know. I guess they must be right. I guess I am psycho. I guess I must be. I must be. Did you ever have ideas like that?"

"No."

"Would they bother you if you did, if you happened to keep imagining a man's head on a woman's body, or if sometimes the arm of a chair turned into a human arm if you looked at it too long, things like that? Would they bother you?"

I didn't say anything.

"Maybe everybody imagines things like that when they're away from home, really far away, for the first time. Do you think so? The camp I went to first, they called it a 'Reception center,' got us up every morning when it was pitch black, and there was food like the kind we throw out here, and all my clothes were gone and I got this uniform that didn't even smell familiar. All day I wanted to sleep, after we got to Basic Training. I kept falling asleep, all day long, at the lectures we went to, and on the firing range, and everywhere else. But not at night. Next to me there was a man who had a cough that sounded like his stomach was going to come up, one of these times, it sounded like it would come up through his mouth and land with a splatter on the floor. He always faced my way. We did sleep head to foot, but I knew it would land near me. I never slept at night. During the day I couldn't eat this food that should have been thrown away, so I was always hungry except in the Mess Hall. The Mess Hall. The army has the perfect word for everything, did you ever think of that?"

I imperceptibly nodded and shook my head, yes-and-no.

"And the perfect word for me," he added in a distorted voice, as though his tongue had swollen, "psycho. I guess I am. I must be. Am I, though, or is

the army? Because they turned everything inside out.
I couldn't sleep in bed, I had to sleep everywhere else.
I couldn't eat in the Mess Hall, I had to eat everywhere else. Everything began to be inside out. And
the man next to me at night, coughing himself inside
out. That was when things began to change. One day
I couldn't make out what was happening to the cor-
poral's face. It kept changing into faces I knew from
somewhere else, and then I began to think he looked
like me, and then he . . ." Leper's voice had thickened
unrecognizably, "he changed into a woman, I was looking at him as close as I'm looking at you and his face
turned into a woman's face and I started to yell for
everybody, I began to yell so that everyone would see
it too, I didn't want to be the only one to see a thing
like that, I yelled louder and louder to make sure
everyone within reach of my voice would hear—you
can see there wasn't anything crazy in the way I was
thinking, can't you, I had a good reason for everything
I did, didn't I—but I couldn't yell soon enough, or loud
enough, and when somebody did finally come up to
me, it was this man with the cough who slept in the
next cot, and he was holding a broom because we had
been sweeping out the barracks, but I saw right away
that it wasn't a broom, it was a man's leg which had
been cut off. I remember thinking that he must have
been at the hospital helping with an amputation when
he heard my yell. You can see there's logic in that."
The crust beneath us continued to crack and as we
reached the border of the field the frigid trees also
were cracking with the cold. The two sharp groups of
noises sounded to my ears like rifles being fired in the
distance.

I said nothing, and Leper, having said so much,
went on to say more, to speak above the wind and

crackings as though his story would never be finished. "Then they grabbed me and there were arms and legs and heads everywhere and I couldn't tell when any minute—"

"*Shut up!*"

Softer, more timidly, "—when any minute—"

"Do you think I want to hear every gory detail! Shut up! I don't care! I don't care what happened to you, Leper. I don't give a damn! Do you understand that? This has nothing to do with me! Nothing at all! I don't care!"

I turned around and began a clumsy run across the field in a line which avoided his house and aimed toward the road leading back into the town. I left Leper telling his story into the wind. He might tell it forever, I didn't care. I didn't want to hear any more of it. I had already heard too much. What did he mean by telling me a story like that! I didn't want to hear any more of it. Not now or ever. I didn't care because it had nothing to do with me. And I didn't want to hear any more of it. Ever.

11

I wanted to see Phineas, and Phineas only. With him there was no conflict except between athletes, something Greek-inspired and Olympian in which victory would go to whoever was the strongest in body and heart. This was the only conflict he had ever believed in.

When I got back I found him in the middle of a snowball fight in a place called the Fields Beyond. At Devon the open ground among the buildings had been given carefully English names—the Center Common, the Far Common, the Fields, and the Fields Beyond. These last were past the gym, the tennis courts, the river and the stadium, on the edge of the woods which, however English in name, were in my mind primevally American, reaching in unbroken forests far to the north, into the great northern wilderness. I found Finny beside the woods playing and fighting—the two were approximately the same thing to him—and I stood there wondering whether things weren't simpler and better at the northern terminus of these woods, a thousand miles due north into the wilderness, somewhere deep in the Arctic, where the peninsula of trees which began at Devon would end at last in an untouched grove of pine, austere and beautiful.

There is no such grove, I know now, but the morning of my return to Devon I imagined that it might be just over the visible horizon, or the horizon after that.

A few of the fighters paused to yell a greeting at me, but no one broke off to ask about Leper. But I knew it was a mistake for me to stay there; at any moment someone might.

This gathering had obviously been Finny's work. Who else could have inveigled twenty people to the farthest extremity of the school to throw snowballs at each other? I could just picture him, at the end of his ten o'clock class, organizing it with the easy authority which always came into his manner when he had an idea which was particularly preposterous. There they all were now, the cream of the school, the lights and leaders of the senior class, with their high I.Q.'s and expensive shoes, as Brinker had said, pasting each other with snowballs.

I hesitated on the edge of the fight and the edge of the woods, too tangled in my mind to enter either one or the other. So I glanced at my wrist watch, brought my hand dramatically to my mouth as though remembering something urgent and important, repeated the pantomime in case anybody had missed it, and with this tacit explanation started briskly back toward the center of the school. A snowball caught me on the back of the head. Finny's voice followed it. "You're on our side, even if you do have a lousy aim. We need *somebody* else. Even you." He came toward me, without his cane at the moment, his new walking cast so much smaller and lighter that an ordinary person could have managed it with hardly a limp noticeable. Finny's coordination, however, was such that any slight flaw became obvious; there was an interruption, brief as a drum beat, in the continuous flow of his walk, as though with each step he forgot for a split-second where he was going.

"How's Leper?" he asked in an offhand way.

"Oh Leper's—how would he be? You know Leper—" The fight was moving toward us; I stalled a little more, a stray snowball caught Finny on the side of the face, he shot one back, I seized some ammunition from the ground and we were engulfed.

Someone knocked me down; I pushed Brinker over a small slope; someone was trying to tackle me from behind. Everywhere there was the smell of vitality in clothes, the vital something in wool and flannel and corduroy which spring releases. I had forgotten that this existed, this smell which instead of the first robin, or the first bud or leaf, means to me that spring has come. I had always welcomed vitality and energy and warmth radiating from thick and sturdy winter clothes. It made me happy, but I kept wondering about next spring, about whether khaki, or suntans or whatever the uniform of the season was, had this aura of promise in it. I felt fairly sure it didn't.

The fight veered. Finny had recruited me and others as allies, so that two sides fighting it out had been taking form. Suddenly he turned his fire against me, he betrayed several of his other friends; he went over to the other, to Brinker's side for a short time, enough to ensure that his betrayal of them would heighten the disorder. Loyalties became hopelessly entangled. No one was going to win or lose after all. Somewhere in the maze Brinker's sense of generalship disappeared, and he too became as slippery as an Arab, as intriguing as a eunuch. We ended the fight in the only way possible; all of us turned on Phineas. Slowly, with a steadily widening grin, he was driven down beneath a blizzard of snowballs.

When he had surrendered I bent cheerfully over to help him up, seizing his wrist to stop the final treacherous snowball he had ready, and he remarked, "Well I guess that takes care of the Hitler Youth outing for one day." All of us laughed. On the way back to the gym he said, "That was a good fight. I thought it was pretty funny, didn't you?"

Hours later it occurred to me to ask him, "Do you think you ought to get into fights like that? After all, there's your leg—"

"Stanpole said something about not falling again, but I'm very careful."

"Christ, don't break it again!"

"No, of course I won't break it again. Isn't the bone supposed to be stronger when it grows together over a place where it's been broken once?"

"Yes, I think it is."

"I think so too. In fact I think I can feel it getting stronger."

"You think you can? Can you feel it?"

"Yes, I think so."

"Thank God."

"What?"

"I said that's good."

"Yes, I guess it is. I guess that's good, all right."

After dinner that night Brinker came to our room to pay us one of his formal calls. Our room had by this time of year the exhausted look of a place where two people had lived too long without taking any interest in their surroundings. Our cots at either end of the room were sway-backed beneath their pink and brown cotton spreads. The walls, which were much farther off white than normal, expressed two forgotten interests: Finny had scotch-taped newspaper pictures of the Roosevelt-Churchill meeting above his cot ("They're the two most important of the old men," he had explained, "getting together to make up what to tell us next about the war"). Over my cot I had long ago taped pictures which together amounted to a bare-faced lie about my background—weepingly romantic views of plantation mansions, moss-hung trees by moonlight, lazy roads winding dustily past the cabins of the Negroes. When asked about them I had acquired an accent appropriate to a town three states south of my own, and I had transmitted the impression, without actually stating it, that this was the old family place. But by now I no longer needed this vivid false identity; now I was acquiring, I felt, a sense of my own real authority and worth, I had had many new experiences and I was growing up.

"How's Leper?" said Brinker as he came in.

"Yeah," said Phineas, "I meant to ask you before."

"Leper? Why he's—he's on leave." But my resentment against having to mislead people seemed to be growing stronger every day. "As a matter of fact Leper is 'Absent Without Leave,' he just took off by himself."

"Leper?" both of them exclaimed together.

"Yes," I shrugged, "Leper. Leper's not the little rabbit we used to know any more."

"Nobody can change *that* much," said Brinker in his new tough-minded way.

Finny said, "He just didn't like the army, I bet. Why should he? What's the point of it anyway?"

"Phineas," Brinker said with dignity, "please don't give us your infantile lecture on world affairs at this time." And to me, "He was too scared to stay, wasn't he?"

I narrowed my eyes as though thinking hard about

that. Finally I said, "Yes, I think you could put it that way."

"He panicked."

I didn't say anything.

"He must be out of his mind," said Brinker energetically, "to do a thing like that. I'll bet he cracked up, didn't he? That's what happened. Leper found out that the army was just too much for him. I've heard about guys like that. Some morning they don't get out of bed with everybody else. They just lie there crying. I'll bet something like that happened to Leper." He looked at me. "Didn't it?"

"Yes. It did."

Brinker had closed with such energy, almost enthusiasm, on the truth that I gave it to him without many misgivings. The moment he had it he crumbled. "Well I'll be damned. I'll be damned. Old Leper. Quiet old Leper. Quiet old Leper from Vermont. He never could fight worth a damn. You'd think somebody would have realized that when he tried to enlist. Poor old Leper. What's he act like?"

"He cries a lot of the time."

"Oh God. What's the matter with our class anyway? It isn't even June yet and we've already got two men sidelined for the Duration."

"Two?"

Brinker hesitated briefly. "Well there's Finny here."

"Yes," agreed Phineas in his deepest and most musical tone, "there's me."

"Finny isn't out of it," I said.

"Of course he is."

"Yes, I'm out of it."

"Not that there's anything to be out of!" I wondered if my face matched the heartiness of my voice. "Just this dizzy war, this fake, this thing with the old men making . . ." I couldn't help watching Finny as I spoke, and so I ran out of momentum. I waited for him to take it up, to unravel once again his tale of plotting statesmen and deluded public, his great joke, his private toe hold on the world. He was sitting on his cot, elbows on knees, looking down. He brought his wide-set eyes up, his grin flashed and faded, and then he murmured, "Sure. There isn't any war."

It was one of the few ironic remarks Phineas ever made, and with it he quietly brought to a close all his special inventions which had carried us through the winter. Now the facts were re-established, and gone were all the fantasies, such as the Olympic Games for A.D. 1944, closed before they had ever been opened.

There was little left at Devon any more which had not been recruited for the war. The few stray activities and dreamy people not caught up in it were being systematically corralled by Brinker. And every day in chapel there was some announcement about qualifying for "V-12," an officer-training program the Navy had set up in many colleges and universities. It sounded very safe, almost like peacetime, almost like just going normally on to college. It was also very popular; groups the size of LST crews joined it, almost everyone who could qualify, except for a few who "wanted to fly" and so chose the Army Air Force, or something called V-5 instead. There were also a special few with energetic fathers who were expecting appointments to Annapolis or West Point or the Coast Guard Academy or even—this alternative had been unexpectedly stumbled on—the Merchant Marine Academy. Devon was by tradition and choice the most civilian of schools, and there was a certain strained hospitality in the way both the faculty and students worked to get along with the leathery recruiting officers who kept appearing on the campus. There was no latent snobbery in us; we didn't find any in them. It was only that we could feel a deep and sincere difference between us and them, a difference which everyone struggled with awkward fortitude to bridge. It was as though Athens and Sparta were trying to establish not just a truce but an alliance—although we were not as civilized as Athens and they were not as brave as Sparta.

Neither were we. There was no rush to get into the fighting; no one seemed to feel the need to get into the infantry, and only a few were talking about the Marines. The thing to be was careful and self-preserving. It was going to be a long war. Quackenbush, I heard, had two possible appointments to the Military Academy, with carefully prepared positions in V-12 and dentistry school to fall back on if necessary.

I myself took no action. I didn't feel free to, and I didn't know why this was so. Brinker, in his accelerating change from absolute to relative virtue, came up with plan after plan, each more insulated from the fighting than the last. But I did nothing.

One morning, after a Naval officer had turned many heads in chapel with an address on convoy duty, Brinker put his hand on the back of my neck in the vestibule outside and steered me into a room used for piano practice near the entrance. It was soundproofed, and he swung the vaultlike door closed behind us.

"You've been putting off enlisting in something for only one reason," he said at once. "You know that, don't you?"

"No, I don't know that."

"Well, I know, and I'll tell you what it is. It's Finny. You pity him."

"Pity him!"

"Yes, pity him. And if you don't watch out he's going to start pitying himself. Nobody ever mentions his leg to him except me. Keep that up and he'll be sloppy with self-pity any day now. What's everybody beating around the bush for? He's crippled and that's that. He's got to accept it and unless we start acting perfectly natural about it, even kid him about it once in a while, he never will."

"You're so wrong I can't even— I can't even *hear* you, you're so wrong."

"Well, I'm going to do it anyway."

"No. You're not."

"The hell I'm not. I don't have to have your approval, do I?"

"I'm his roommate, and I'm his best friend—"

"And you were there when it happened. I know. And I don't give a damn. And don't forget," he looked at me sharply, "you've got a little personal stake in this. What I mean is it wouldn't do you any harm, you know, if everything about Finny's accident was cleared up and forgotten."

I felt my face grimacing in the way Finny's did when he was really irritated. "What do you mean by that?"

"I don't know," he shrugged and chuckled in his best manner, "nobody knows." Then the charm disappeared and he added, "unless you know," and his mouth closed in its straight expressionless line, and that was all that was said.

I had no idea what Brinker might say or do. Before he had always known and done whatever occurred to him because he was certain that whatever occurred to him was right. In the world of the Golden Fleece Debating Society and the Underprivileged Local Children subcommittee of the Good Samaritan Confraternity, this had created no problems. But I was afraid of that simple executive directness now.

I walked back from Chapel and found Finny in our dormitory, blocking the staircase until the others who wanted to go up sang *A Mighty Fortress Is Our God* under his direction. No one who was tone deaf ever loved music so much. I think his shortcoming increased his appreciation; he loved it all indiscriminately— Beethoven, the latest love ditty, jazz, a hymn—it was all profoundly musical to Phineas.

" . . . Our helper He a-mid the floods," wafted out across the Common in the tempo of a football march, "Of mortal ills prevailing!"

"Everything was all right," said Finny at the end, "phrasing, rhythm, all that. But I'm not sure about your pitch. Half a tone off, I would estimate offhand."

We went on to our room. I sat down at the translation of Caesar I was doing for him, since he had to pass Latin at last this year or fail to graduate. I thought I was doing a pretty good job of it.

"Is anything exciting happening now?"

"This part is pretty interesting," I said, "if I understand it right. About a surprise attack."

"Read me that."

"Well let's see. It begins, 'When Caesar noticed that the enemy was remaining for several days at the camp fortified by a swamp and by the nature of the terrain, he sent a letter to Trebonius instructing him'—'instructing him' isn't actually in the text but it's understood; you know about that."

"Sure. Go on."

"'Instructing him to come as quickly as possible by long forced marches to him'—this 'him' refers to Caesar of course."

Finny looked at me with glazed interest and said, "Of course."

"'Instructing him to come as quickly as possible by long forced marches to him with three legions; he himself'—Caesar, that is—'sent cavalry to withstand any sudden attacks of the enemy. Now when the Gauls learned what was going on, they scattered a selected band of foot soldiers in ambushes; who, overtaking our horsemen after the leader Vertiscus had been killed, followed our disorderly men up to our camp.'"

"I have a feeling that's what Mr. Horn is going to call a 'muddy translation.' What's it mean?"

"Caesar isn't doing so well."

"But he won it in the end."

"Sure. If you mean the whole campaign—" I broke off. "He won it, if you really think there was a Gallic War . . ." Caesar, from the first, had been the one historical figure Phineas refused absolutely to believe in. Lost two thousand years in the past, master of a dead language and a dead empire, the bane and bore of schoolboys, Caesar he believed to be more of a tyrant at Devon than he had ever been in Rome. Phineas felt a personal and sincere grudge against Caesar, and he was outraged most by his conviction that Caesar and Rome and Latin had never been alive at all . . . "If you really think there ever was a Caesar," I said.

Finny got up from the cot, picking up his cane as an afterthought. He looked oddly at me, his face set to burst out laughing I thought. "Naturally I don't believe books and I don't believe teachers," he came across a few paces, "but I do believe—it's important after all for me to believe *you*. Christ, I've got to be-

lieve you, at least. I know you better than anybody."
I waited without saying anything. "And you told me
about Leper, that he's gone crazy. That's the word,
we might as well admit it. Leper's gone crazy. When
I heard that about Leper, then I knew that the war
was real, this war and all the wars. If a war can drive
somebody crazy, then it's real all right. Oh I guess I
always *knew*, but I didn't have to admit it." He
perched his foot, small cast with metal bar across the
bottom to walk on, next to where I was sitting on the
cot. "To tell you the truth, I wasn't too completely
sure about *you*, when you told me how Leper was.
Of course I believed you," he added hurriedly, "but
you're the nervous type, you know, and I thought
maybe your imagination got a little inflamed up there
in Vermont. I thought he might not be quite as mixed
up as you made out." Finny's face tried to prepare me
for what came next. "Then I saw him myself."

I turned incredulously. "You saw Leper?"

"I saw him here this morning, after chapel. He was
—well, there's nothing inflamed about my imagination
and I saw Leper *hiding* in the shrubbery next to the
chapel. I slipped out the side door the way I always
do—to miss the rush—and I saw Leper and he must
have seen me. He didn't say a damn word. He looked
at me like I was a gorilla or something and then he
ducked into Mr. Carhart's office."

"He must be crazy," I said automatically, and then
my eyes involuntarily met Finny's. We both broke into
sudden laughter.

"We can't do a damn thing about it," he said rue-
fully.

"I don't want to see him," I muttered. Then, trying
to be more responsible, "Who else knows he's here."

"No one, I would think."

"There's nothing for us to do, maybe Carhart or Dr. Stanpole can do something. We won't tell anybody about it because . . . because they would just scare Leper, and he would scare them."

"Anyway," said Finny, "then I knew there was a real war on."

"Yes, I guess it's a real war all right. But I liked yours a lot better."

"So did I."

"I wish you hadn't found out. What did you have to find out for!" We started to laugh again, with a half-guilty exchange of glances, in the way that two people who had gone on a gigantic binge when they were last together would laugh when they met again at the parson's tea. "Well," he said, "you did a beautiful job in the Olympics."

"And you were the greatest news analyst who ever lived."

"Do you realize you won every gold medal in every Olympic event? No one's ever done anything like that in history."

"And you scooped every newspaper in the world on every story." The sun was doing antics among the million specks of dust hanging between us and casting a brilliant, unstable pool of light on the floor. "No one's ever done anything like that before."

Brinker and three cohorts came with much commotion into our room at 10:05 P.M. that night. "We're taking you out," he said flatly.

"It's after hours," I said; "Where?" said Finny with interest at the same time.

"You'll see. Get them." His friends half-lifted us half-roughly, and we were hustled down the stairs. I thought it must be some kind of culminating prank,

the senior class leaving Devon with a flourish. Were
we going to steal the clapper of the school bell, or
would we tether a cow in chapel?

They steered us toward the First Building—burned
down and rebuilt several times but still known as the
First Building of the Devon School. It contained only
classrooms and so at this hour was perfectly empty,
which made us stealthier than ever. Brinker's many
keys, surviving from his class-officer period, jingled
softly as we reached the main door. Above us in Latin
flowed the inscription, Here Boys Come to Be Made
Men.

The lock turned; we went in, entering the doubtful
reality of a hallway familiar only in daylight and
bustle. Our footsteps fell guiltily on the marble floor.
We continued across the foyer to a dreamlike bank
of windows, turned left up a pale flight of marble
steps, left again, through two doorways, and into the
Assembly Room. From the high ceiling one of the
celebrated Devon chandeliers, all glittering tears, scattered thin illumination. Row after row of black Early
American benches spread emptily back through the
shadows to long, vague windows. At the front of the
room there was a raised platform with a balustrade in
front of it. About ten members of the senior class sat
on the platform; all of them were wearing their black
graduation robes. This is going to be some kind of
schoolboy masquerade, I thought, some masquerade
with masks and candles.

"You see how Phineas limps," said Brinker loudly as
we walked in. It was too coarse and too loud; I wanted
to hit him for shocking me like that. Phineas looked
perplexed. "Sit down," he went on, "take a load off
your feet." We sat in the front row of the benches

where eight or ten others were sitting, smirking uneasily at the students on the platform.

Whatever Brinker had in his mind to do, I thought he had chosen a terrible place for it. There was nothing funny about the Assembly Room. I could remember staring torpidly through these windows a hundred times out at the elms of the Center Common. The windows now had the closed blankness of night, a deadened look about them, a look of being blind or deaf. The great expanses of wall space were opaque with canvas, portraits in oil of deceased headmasters, a founder or two, forgotten leaders of the faculty, a beloved athletic coach none of us had ever heard of, a lady we could not identify—her fortune had largely rebuilt the school; a nameless poet who was thought when under the school's protection to be destined primarily for future generations; a young hero now anonymous who looked theatrical in the First World War uniform in which he had died.

I thought any prank was bound to fall flat here.

The Assembly Hall was used for large lectures, debates, plays, and concerts; it had the worst acoustics in the school. I couldn't make out what Brinker was saying. He stood on the polished marble floor in front of us, but facing the platform, talking to the boys behind the balustrade. I heard him say the word "inquiry" to them, and something about "the country demands. . . ."

"What is all this hot air?" I said into the blur.

"I don't know," Phineas answered shortly.

As he turned toward us Brinker was saying ". . . blame on the responsible party. We will begin with a brief prayer." He paused, surveying us with the kind of wide-eyed surmise Mr. Carhart always used at this point, and then added in Mr. Carhart's urbane murmur, "Let us pray."

We all slumped immediately and unthinkingly into the awkward crouch in which God was addressed at Devon, leaning forward with elbows on knees. Brinker had caught us, and in a moment it was too late to escape, for he had moved swiftly into the Lord's Prayer. If when Brinker had said "Let us pray" I had said "Go to hell" everything might have been saved.

At the end there was an indecisive, semiserious silence and then Brinker said, "Phineas, if you please." Finny got up with a shrug and walked to the center of the floor, between us and the platform. Brinker got an armchair from behind the balustrade, and seated Finny on it with courtly politeness. "Now just in your own words," he said.

"What own words?" said Phineas, grimacing up at him with his best you-are-an-idiot expression.

"I know you haven't got many of your own," said Brinker with a charitable smile. "Use some of Gene's then."

"What shall I talk about? You? I've got plenty of words of my own for that."

"*I'm* all right," Brinker glanced gravely around the room for confirmation, "you're the casualty."

"Brinker," began Finny in a constricted voice I did not recognize, "are you off your head or what?"

"No," said Brinker evenly, "that's Leper, our other casualty. Tonight we're investigating you."

"What the hell are you talking about!" I cut in suddenly.

"Investigating Finny's accident!" He spoke as though this was the most natural and self-evident and inevitable thing we could be doing.

I felt the blood flooding into my head. "After all,"

Brinker continued, "there *is* a war on. Here's one soldier our side has already lost. We've got to find out what happened."

"Just for the record," said someone from the platform. "You agree, don't you, Gene?"

"I told Brinker this morning," I began in a voice treacherously shaking, "that I thought this was the worst—"

"And I said," Brinker's voice was full of authority and perfectly under control, "that for Finny's good," and with an additional timbre of sincerity, "and for your own good too, by the way, Gene, that we should get all this out into the open. We don't want any mysteries or any stray rumors and suspicions left in the air at the end of the year, do we?"

A collective assent to this rumbled through the blurring atmosphere of the Assembly Room.

"What are you talking about!" Finny's voice was full of contemptuous music. "What rumors and suspicions?"

"Never mind about that," said Brinker with his face responsibly grave. He's enjoying this, I thought bitterly, he's imagining himself Justice incarnate, balancing the scales. He's forgotten that Justice incarnate is not only balancing the scales but also blindfolded. "Why don't you just tell us in your words what happened?" Brinker continued. "Just humor us, if you want to think of it that way. We aren't trying to make you feel bad. Just tell us. You know we wouldn't ask you if we didn't have a good reason . . . good reasons."

"There's nothing to tell."

"Nothing to tell?" Brinker looked pointedly at the small cast around Finny's lower leg and the cane he held between his knees.

"Well then, I fell out of a tree."

"Why?" said someone on the platform. The acoustics were so bad and the light so dim that I could rarely tell who was speaking, except for Finny and Brinker who were isolated on the wide strip of marble floor between us in the seats and the others on the platform.

"Why?" repeated Phineas. "Because I took a wrong step."

"Did you lose your balance?" continued the voice.

"Yes," echoed Finny grimly, "I lost my balance."

"You had better balance than anyone in the school."

"Thanks a lot."

"I didn't say it for a compliment."

"Well then, no thanks."

"Have you ever thought that you didn't just fall out of that tree?"

This touched an interesting point Phineas had been turning over in his mind for a long time. I could tell that because the obstinate, competitive look left his face as his mind became engaged for the first time. "It's very funny," he said, "but ever since then I've had a feeling that the tree did it by itself. It's an impression I've had. Almost as though the tree shook me out by itself."

The acoustics in the Assembly Room were so poor that silences there had a heavy hum of their own.

"Someone else was in the tree, isn't that so?"

"No," said Finny spontaneously, "I don't think so." He looked at the ceiling. "Or was there? Maybe there was somebody climbing up the rungs of the trunk. I kind of forget."

This time the hum of silence was prolonged to a point where I would be forced to fill it with some kind of sound if it didn't end. Then someone else on the platform spoke up. "I thought somebody told me that Gene Forrester was—"

"Finny was there," Brinker interrupted commandingly, "he knows better than anyone."

"You were there too, weren't you, Gene?" this new voice from the platform continued.

"Yes," I said with interest, "yes, I was there too."

"Were you—near the tree?"

Finny turned toward me. "You were down at the bottom, weren't you?" he asked, not in the official courtroom tone he had used before, but in a friend's voice.

I had been studying very carefully the way my hands wrinkled when tightly clenched, but I was able to bring my head up and return his inquiring look. "Down at the bottom, yes."

Finny went on. "Did you see the tree shake or anything?" He flushed faintly at what seemed to him the absurdity of his own question. "I've always meant to ask you, just for the hell of it."

I took this under consideration. "I don't recall anything like that . . ."

"Nutty question," he muttered.

"I thought you were in the tree," the platform voice cut in.

"Well of course," Finny said with an exasperated chuckle, "of course *I* was in the tree—oh you mean Gene?—he wasn't in—is that what you mean, or—" Finny floundered with muddled honesty between me and my questioner.

"I meant Gene," the voice said.

"Of course Finny was in the tree," I said. But I couldn't make the confusion last, "and I was down at the bottom, or climbing the rungs I think . . ."

"How do you expect him to remember?" said Finny sharply. "There was a hell of a lot of confusion right then."

"A kid I used to play with was hit by a car once when I was about eleven years old," said Brinker seriously, "and I remember every single thing about it, exactly where I was standing, the color of the sky, the noise the brakes of the car made—I never will forget anything about it."

"You and I are two different people," I said.

"No one's accusing you of anything," Brinker responded in an odd tone.

"Well of course no one's *accusing* me—"

"Don't argue so much," his voice tried for a hard compromise, full of warning and yet striving to pass unnoticed by the others.

"No, we're not accusing you," a boy on the platform said evenly, and then I stood accused.

"I think I remember now!" Finny broke in, his eyes bright and relieved. "Yes, I remember seeing you standing on the bank. You were looking up and your hair was plastered down over your forehead so that you had that dumb look you always have when you've been in the water—what was it you said? 'Stop posing up there' or one of those best-pal cracks you're always making." He was very happy. "And I think I did start to pose just to make you madder, and I said, what did I say? something about the two of us . . . yes, I said 'Let's make a double jump,' because I thought if we went together it would be something that had never been done before, holding hands in a jump—" Then it was as though someone suddenly slapped him. "No, that was on the ground when I said that to you. I said that to you on the ground, and then the two of us started to climb . . ." he broke off.

"The two of you," the boy on the platform went on harshly for him, "started to climb up the tree together, was that it? And he's just said he was on the ground!"

"Or on the rungs!" I burst out. "I said I might have been on the rungs!"

"Who else was there?" said Brinker quietly. "Leper Lepellier was there, wasn't he?"

"Yes," someone said, "Leper was there."

"Leper always was the exact type when it came to details," continued Brinker. "He could have told us where everybody was standing, what everybody was wearing, the whole conversation that day, and what the temperature was. He could have cleared the whole thing up. Too bad."

No one said anything. Phineas had been sitting motionless, leaning slightly forward, not far from the position in which we prayed at Devon. After a long time he turned and reluctantly looked at me. I did not return his look or move or speak. Then at last Finny straightened from this prayerful position slowly, as though it was painful for him. "Leper's here," he said in a voice so quiet, and with such quiet unconscious dignity, that he was suddenly terrifyingly strange to me. "I saw him go into Dr. Carhart's office this morning."

"Here! Go get him," said Brinker immediately to the two boys who had come with us. "He must be in Carhart's rooms if he hasn't gone back home."

I kept quiet. To myself, however, I made a number of swift, automatic calculations: that Leper was no threat, no one would ever believe Leper; Leper was deranged, he was not of sound mind and if people couldn't make out their own wills when not in sound mind certainly they couldn't testify in something like this.

The two boys left and the atmosphere immediately cleared. Action had been taken, so the whole issue was dropped for now. Someone began making fun of "Cap-

tain Marvel," the head of the football team, saying
how girlish he looked in his graduation gown. Captain
Marvel minced for us in his size 12 shoes, the sides
of his gown swaying drunkenly back and forth from
his big hips. Someone wound himself in the folds of
the red velvet curtain and peered out from it like an
exotic spy. Someone made a long speech listing every
infraction of the rules we were committing that night.
Someone else made a speech showing how by careful
planning we could break all the others before dawn.

But although the acoustics in the Assembly Hall
were poor, those outside the room were admirable.
All the talk and horseplay ended within a few seconds
of the instant when the first person, that is myself,
heard the footsteps returning along the marble stairway and corridors toward us. I knew with absolute
certainty moments before they came in that there were
three sets of footsteps coming.

Leper entered ahead of the other two. He looked
unusually well; his face was glowing, his eyes were
bright, his manner was all energy. "Yes?" he said in
a clear voice, resonant even in this room, "what can
I do for you?" He made this confident remark almost
but not quite to Phineas, who was still sitting alone
in the middle of the room. Finny muttered something
which was too indecisive for Leper, who turned with
a cleanly energetic gesture toward Brinker. Brinker
began talking to him in the elaborately casual manner
of someone being watched. Gradually the noise in the
room, which had revived when the three of them came
in, subsided again.

Brinker managed it. He never raised his voice, but
instead he let the noise surrounding it gradually sink
so that his voice emerged in the ensuing silence without any emphasis on his part—"so that you were stand-

ing next to the river bank, watching Phineas climb the tree?" he was saying, and had waited, I knew, until this silence to say.

"Sure. Right there by the trunk of the tree. I was looking up. It was almost sunset, and I remember the way the sun was shining in my eyes."

"So you couldn't . . ." I began before I could stop myself.

There was a short pause during which every ear and no eyes were directed toward me, and then Brinker went on. "And what did you see? Could you see anything with the sun in your eyes?"

"Oh sure," said Leper in his new, confident, false voice. "I just shaded my eyes a little, like this," he demonstrated how a hand shades the eyes, "and then I could see. I could see both of them clearly enough because the sun was blazing all around them," a certain singsong sincerity was developing in his voice, as though he were trying to hold the interest of young children, "and the rays of the sun were shooting past them, millions of rays shooting past them like—like golden machine-gun fire." He paused to let us consider the profoundly revealing exactness of this phrase. "That's what it was like, if you want to know. The two of them looked as black as—as black as death standing up there with this fire burning all around them."

Everyone could hear, couldn't they? the derangement in his voice. Everyone must be able to see how false his confidence was. Any fool could see that. But whatever I said would be a self-indictment; others would have to fight for me.

"Up there where?" said Brinker brusquely. "Where were the two of them standing up there?"

"On the limb!" Leper's annoyed, this-is-obvious tone

would discount what he said in their minds; they would know that he had never been like this before, that he had changed and was not responsible.

"Who was where on the limb? Was one of them ahead of the other?"

"Well of course."

"Who was ahead?"

Leper smiled waggishly. "I couldn't see *that*. There were just two shapes, and with that fire shooting past them they looked as black as—"

"You've already told us that. You couldn't see who was ahead?"

"No, naturally I couldn't."

"But you could see how they were standing. Where were they exactly?"

"One of them was next to the trunk, holding the trunk of the tree. I'll never forget that because the tree was a huge black shape too, and his hand touching the black trunk anchored him, if you see what I mean, to something solid in all the bright fire they were standing in up there. And the other one was a little farther out on the limb."

"Then what happened?"

"Then they both moved."

"How did they move?"

"They moved," now Leper was smiling, a charming and slightly arch smile, like a child who knows he is going to say something clever, "they moved like an engine."

In the baffled silence I began to uncoil slowly.

"Like an engine!" Brinker's expression was a struggle between surprise and disgust.

"I can't think of the name of the engine. But it has two pistons. What is that engine? Well anyway, in this engine first one piston sinks, and then the next one sinks. The one holding on to the trunk sank for a second, up and down like a piston, and then the other one sank and fell."

Someone on the platform exclaimed, "The one who moved first shook the other one's balance!"

"I suppose so." Leper seemed to be rapidly losing interest.

"Was the one who fell," Brinker said slowly, "was Phineas, in other words the one who moved first or second?"

Leper's face became guileful, his voice flat and impersonal. "I don't intend to implicate myself. I'm no fool, you know. I'm not going to tell you everything and then have it used against me later. You always did take me for a fool, didn't you? But I'm no fool any more. I know when I have information that might be dangerous." He was working himself up to indignation. "Why should I tell you! Just because it happens to suit you!"

"Leper," Brinker pleaded, "Leper, this is very important—"

"So am I," he said thinly, "I'm important. You've never realized it, but I'm important too. You be the fool," he gazed shrewdly at Brinker, "you do whatever anyone wants whenever they want it. You be the fool now. Bastard."

Phineas had gotten up unnoticed from his chair. "I don't care," he interrupted in an even voice, so full of richness that it overrode all the others. "I don't care."

I tore myself from the bench toward him. "Phineas—!"

He shook his head sharply, closing his eyes, and then he turned to regard me with a handsome mask of face. "I just don't care. Never mind," and he started across the marble floor toward the doors.

"Wait a minute!" cried Brinker. "We haven't heard everything yet. We haven't got all the facts!"

The words shocked Phineas into awareness. He whirled as though being attacked from behind. "You get the rest of the facts, Brinker!" he cried. "You get all your facts!" I had never seen Finny crying, "You collect every f——ing fact there is in the world!" He plunged out the doors.

The excellent exterior acoustics recorded his rushing steps and the quick rapping of his cane along the corridor and on the first steps of the marble stairway. Then these separate sounds collided into the general tumult of his body falling clumsily down the white marble stairs.

12

Everyone behaved with complete presence of mind. Brinker shouted that Phineas must not be moved; someone else, realizing that only a night nurse would be at the Infirmary, did not waste time going there but rushed to bring Dr. Stanpole from his house. Others remembered that Phil Latham, the wrestling coach, lived just across the Common and that he was an expert in first aid. It was Phil who made Finny stretch out on one of the wide shallow steps of the staircase, and kept him still until Dr. Stanpole arrived.

The foyer and the staircase of the First Building were soon as crowded as at midday. Phil Latham found the main light switch, and all the marble blazed up under full illumination. But surrounding it was the stillness of near-midnight in a country town, so that the hurrying feet and the repressed voices had a hollow reverberance. The windows, blind and black, retained their look of dull emptiness.

Once Brinker turned to me and said, "Go back to the Assembly Room and see if there's any kind of blanket on the platform." I dashed back up the stairs, found a blanket and gave it to Phil Latham. He carefully wrapped it around Phineas.

I would have liked very much to have done that

myself; it would have meant a lot to me. But Phineas might begin to curse me with every word he knew, he might lose his head completely, he would certainly be worse off for it. So I kept out of the way.

He was entirely conscious and from the glimpses I caught of his face seemed to be fairly calm. Everyone behaved with complete presence of mind, and that included Phineas.

When Dr. Stanpole arrived there was silence on the stairs. Wrapped tightly in his blanket, with light flooding down on him from the chandelier, Finny lay isolated at the center of a tight circle of faces. The rest of the crowd looked on from above or below on the stairs, and I stood on the lower edge. Behind me the foyer was now empty.

After a short, silent examination Dr. Stanpole had a chair brought from the Assembly Room, and Finny was lifted cautiously into it. People aren't ordinarily carried in chairs in New Hampshire, and as they raised him up he looked very strange to me, like some tragic and exalted personage, a stricken pontiff. Once again I had the desolating sense of having all along ignored what was finest in him. Perhaps it was just the incongruity of seeing him aloft and stricken, since he was by nature someone who carried others. I didn't think he knew how to act or even how to feel as the object of help. He went past with his eyes closed and his mouth tense. I knew that normally I would have been one of those carrying the chair, saying something into his ear as we went along. My aid alone had never seemed to him in the category of help. The reason for this occurred to me as the procession moved slowly across the brilliant foyer to the doors; Phineas had thought of me as an extension of himself.

Dr. Stanpole stopped near the doors, looking for the

light switch. There was an interval of a few seconds
when no one was near him. I came up to him and
tried to phrase my question but nothing came out, I
couldn't find the word to begin. I was being torn irre-
concilably between "Is he" and "What is" when Dr.
Stanpole, without appearing to notice my tangle, said
conversationally, "It's the leg again. Broken again. But
a much cleaner break I think, much cleaner. A simple
fracture." He found the light switch and the foyer was
plunged into darkness.

Outside, the doctor's car was surrounded by boys
while Finny was being lifted inside it by Phil Latham.
Phil and Dr. Stanpole then got into the car and drove
slowly away, the headlights forming a bright parallel
as they receded down the road, and then swinging into
another parallel at right angles to the first as they
turned into the Infirmary driveway. The crowd began
to thin rapidly; the faculty had at last heard that something was amiss in the night, and several alarmed and
alarming masters materialized in the darkness and
ordered the students to their dormitories.

Mr. Ludsbury loomed abruptly out of a background
of shrubbery. "Get along to the dormitory, Forrester,"
he said with a dry certainty in my obedience which
suddenly struck me as funny, definitely funny. Since
it was beneath his dignity to wait and see that I actually followed his order, I was by not budging free of
him a moment later. I walked into the bank of shrubbery, circled past trees in the direction of the chapel,
doubled back along a large building donated by the
alumni which no one had ever been able to put to
use, recrossed the street and walked noiselessly up the
emerging grass next to the Infirmary driveway.

Dr. Stanpole's car was at the top of it, headlights

on and motor running, empty. I idly considered stealing it, in the way that people idly consider many
crimes it would be possible for them to commit. I took
an academic interest in the thought of stealing the car,
knowing all the time that it would be not so much
criminal as meaningless, a lapse into nothing, an escape into nowhere. As I walked past it the motor was
throbbing with wheezy reluctance—prep school doc-
tors don't own very desirable getaway cars, I remember thinking to myself—and then I turned the corner
of the building and began to creep along behind it.
There was only one window lighted, at the far end,
and opposite it I found some thin shrubbery which
provided enough cover for me to study the window.
It was too high for me to see directly into the room,
but after I made sure that the ground had softened
enough so that I could jump without making much
noise, I sprang as high as I could. I had a flashing
glimpse of a door at the other end of the room, opening on the corridor. I jumped again; someone's back.
Again; nothing new. I jumped again and saw a head
and shoulders partially turned away from me; Phil
Latham's. This was the room.

The ground was too damp to sit on, so I crouched
down and waited. I could hear their blurred voices
droning monotonously through the window. If they do
nothing worse, they're going to bore Finny to death,
I said to myself. My head seemed to be full of bright
remarks this evening. It was cold crouching motionless
next to the ground. I stood up and jumped several
times, not so much to see into the room as to warm
up. The only sounds were occasional snorts from the
engine of Dr. Stanpole's car when it turned over with
special reluctance, and a thin, lonely whistling the wind
sometimes made high in the still-bare trees. These

formed the background for the dull hum of talk in Finny's room as Phil Latham, Dr. Stanpole and the night nurse worked over him.

What could they be talking about? The night nurse had always been the biggest windbag in the school. Miss Windbag, R.N. Phil Latham, on the other hand, hardly ever spoke. One of the few things he said was "Give it the old college try"—he thought of everything in terms of the old college try, and he had told students to attack their studies, their sports, religious waverings, sexual maladjustments, physical handicaps and a constellation of other problems with the old college try. I listened tensely for his voice. I listened so hard that I nearly differentiated it from the others, and it seemed to be saying, "Finny, give that bone the old college try."

I was quite a card tonight myself.

Phil Latham's college was Harvard, although I had heard that he only lasted there a year. Probably he had said to someone to give something the old college try, and that had finished him; that would probably be grounds for expulsion at Harvard. There couldn't possibly be such a thing as the old Harvard try. Could there be the old Devon try? The old Devon endeavor? The decrepit Devon endeavor? That was good, the decrepit Devon endeavor. I'd use that some time in the Butt Room. That was pretty funny. I'll bet I could get a rise out of Finny with—

Dr. Stanpole was fairly gabby too. What was he always saying. Nothing. Nothing? Well there must be something he was always saying. Everybody had something, some word, some phrase that they were always saying. The trouble with Dr. Stanpole was that his vocabulary was too large. He talked in a huge circle, he probably had a million words in his vocabulary and he had to use them all before he started over again.

That's probably the way they were talking in there now. Dr. Stanpole was working his way as fast as possible around his big circle, Miss Windbag was gasping out something or other all the time, and Phil Latham was saying, "Give 'er the old college try, Finny." Phineas of course was answering them only in Latin.

I nearly laughed out loud at that.

Gallia est omnis divisa in partes tres—Finny probably answered that whenever Phil Latham spoke. Phil Latham would look rather blank at that.

Did Finny like Phil Latham? Yes, of course he did. But wouldn't it be funny if he suddenly turned to him and said, "Phil Latham, you're a boob." That would be funny in a way. And what about if he said, "Dr. Stanpole, old pal, you're the most long-winded licensed medical man alive." And it would be even funnier if he interrupted that night nurse and said, "Miss Windbag, you're rotten, rotten to the core. I just thought I ought to tell you." It would never occur to Finny to say any of these things, but they struck me as so outrageous that I couldn't stop myself from laughing. I put my hand over my mouth; then I tried to stop my mouth with my fist; if I couldn't get control of this laughing they would hear me in the room. I was laughing so hard it hurt my stomach and I could feel my face getting more and more flushed; I dug my teeth into my fist to try to gain control and then I noticed that there were tears all over my hand.

The engine of Dr. Stanpole's car roared exhaustedly. The headlights turned in an erratic arc away from me, and then I heard the engine laboriously recede into the distance, and I continued to listen until not only had it ceased but my memory of how it sounded had also ceased. The light had gone out in the room and there was no sound coming from it. The only noise was the peculiarly bleak whistling of the wind through the upper branches.

There was a street light behind me somewhere through the trees and the windows of the Infirmary dimly reflected it. I came up close beneath the window of Finny's room, found a foothold on a grating beneath it, straightened up so that my shoulders were at a level with the window sill, reached up with both hands, and since I was convinced that the window would be stuck shut I pushed it hard. The window shot up and there was a startled rustling from the bed in the shadows. I whispered, "Finny!" sharply into the black room.

"Who is it!" he demanded, leaning out from the bed so that the light fell waveringly on his face. Then he recognized me and I thought at first he was going to get out of bed and help me through the window. He struggled clumsily for such a length of time that even my mind, shocked and slowed as it had been, was able to formulate two realizations: that his leg was bound so that he could not move very well, and that he was struggling to unleash his hate against me.

"I came to—"

"You want to break something else in me! Is that why you're here!" He thrashed wildly in the darkness, the bed groaning under him and the sheets hissing as he fought against them. But he was not going to be able to get to me, because his matchless coordination was gone. He could not even get up from the bed.

"I want to fix your leg up," I said crazily but in a perfectly natural tone of voice which made my words sound even crazier, even to me.

"You'll fix my . . ." and he arched out, lunging hopelessly into the space between us. He arched out and then fell, his legs still on the bed, his hands falling with a loud slap against the floor. Then after a pause all the tension drained out of him, and he let his head come slowly down between his hands. He had not hurt himself. But he brought his head slowly down between his hands and rested it against the floor, not moving, not making any sound.

"I'm sorry," I said blindly, "I'm sorry, I'm sorry."

I had just control enough to stay out of his room, to let him struggle back into the bed by himself. I slid down from the window, and I remember lying on the ground staring up at the night sky, which was neither clear nor overcast. And I remember later walking alone down a rather aimless road which leads past the gym to an old water hole. I was trying to cope with something that might be called double vision. I saw the gym in the glow of a couple of outside lights near it and I knew of course that it was the Devon gym which I entered every day. It was and it wasn't. There was something innately strange about it, as though there had always been an inner core to the gym which I had never perceived before, quite different from its generally accepted appearance. It seemed to alter moment by moment before my eyes, becoming for brief flashes a totally unknown building with a significance much deeper and far more real than any I had noticed before. The same was true of the water hole, where unauthorized games of hockey were played during the winter. The ice was breaking up on it now, with just a few glazed islands of ice remaining in the center and a fringe of hard surface glinting along the banks. The old trees surrounding it all were intensely meaningful, with a message that was very pressing and entirely indecipherable. Here the road turned to the

left and became dirt. It proceeded along the lower end
of the playing fields, and under the pale night glow
the playing fields swept away from me in slight frosty
undulations which bespoke meanings upon meanings,
levels of reality I had never suspected before, a kind
of thronging and epic grandeur which my superficial
eyes and cluttered mind had been blind to before.
They unrolled away impervious to me as though I
were a roaming ghost, not only tonight but always, as
though I had never played on them a hundred times,
as though my feet had never touched them, as though
my whole life at Devon had been a dream, or rather
that everything at Devon, the playing fields, the gym,
the water hole, and all the other buildings and all the
people there were intensely real, wildly alive and
totally meaningful, and I alone was a dream, a fig-
ment which had never really touched anything. I felt
that I was not, never had been and never would be a
living part of this overpoweringly solid and deeply
meaningful world around me.

I reached the bridge which arches over the little
Devon River and beyond it the dirt track which curves
toward the stadium. The stadium itself, two white concrete banks of seats, was as powerful and alien to me
as an Aztec ruin, filled with the traces of vanished
people and vanished rites, of supreme emotions and
supreme tragedies. The old phrase about "If these
walls could only speak" occurred to me and I felt it
more deeply than anyone has ever felt it, I felt that the
stadium could not only speak but that its words could
hold me spellbound. In fact the stadium did speak
powerfully and at all times, including this moment.
But I could not hear, and that was because I did not
exist.

I awoke the next morning in a dry and fairly sheltered corner of the ramp underneath the stadium. My neck was stiff from sleeping in an awkward position. The sun was high and the air freshened.

I walked back to the center of the school and had breakfast and then went to my room to get a notebook, because this was Wednesday and I had a class at 9:10. But at the door of the room I found a note from Dr. Stanpole. "Please bring some of Finny's clothes and his toilet things to the Infirmary."

I took his suitcase from the corner where it had been accumulating dust and put what he would need into it. I didn't know what I was going to say at the Infirmary. I couldn't escape a confusing sense of having lived through all of this before—Phineas in the Infirmary, and myself responsible. I seemed to be less shocked by it now than I had the first time last August, when it had broken over our heads like a thunderclap in a flawless sky. There were hints of much worse things around us now like a faint odor in the air, evoked by words like "plasma" and "psycho" and "sulfa," strange words like that with endings like Latin nouns. The newsreels and magazines were choked with images of blazing artillery and bodies half sunk in the sand of a beach somewhere. We members of the Class of 1943 were moving very fast toward the war now, so fast that there were casualties even before we reached it, a mind was clouded and a leg was broken—maybe these should be thought of as minor and inevitable mishaps in the accelerating rush. The air around us was filled with much worse things.

In this way I tried to calm myself as I walked with Finny's suitcase toward the Infirmary. After all, I reflected to myself, people were shooting flames into caves and grilling other people alive, ships were being torpedoed and dropping thousands of men in the icy ocean, whole city blocks were exploding into flame in an instant. My brief burst of animosity, lasting only a second, a part of a second, something which came before I could recognize it and was gone before I knew it had possessed me, what was that in the midst of this holocaust?

I reached the Infirmary with Finny's suitcase and went inside. The air was laden with hospital smells, not unlike those of the gym except that the Infirmary lacked that sense of spent human vitality. This was becoming the new background of Finny's life, this purely medical element from which bodily health was absent.

The corridor happened to be empty, and I walked along it in the grip of a kind of fatal exhilaration. All doubt had been resolved at last. There was a wartime phrase coming into style just then—"this is it"—and although it later became a parody of itself, it had a final flat accuracy which was all that could be said at certain times. This was one of the times: this was it.

I knocked and went in. He was stripped to the waist, sitting up in bed leafing through a magazine. I carried my head low by instinct, and I had the courage for only a short glance at him before I said quietly, "I've brought your stuff."

"Put the suitcase on the bed here, will you?" The tone of his words fell dead center, without a trace of friendliness or unfriendliness, not interested and not bored, not energetic and not languid.

I put it down beside him, and he opened it and began to look through the extra underwear and shirts and socks I had packed. I stood precariously in the middle of the room, trying to find somewhere to look and something to say, wanting desperately to leave and powerless to do so. Phineas went carefully over his clothes, apparently very calm. But it wasn't like him to check with such care, not like him at all. He was taking a long time at it, and then I noticed that as he tried to slide a hairbrush out from under a flap holding it in the case his hands were shaking so badly that he couldn't get it out. Seeing that released me on the spot.

"Finny, I tried to tell you before, I tried to tell you when I came to Boston that time—"

"I know, I remember that." He couldn't, after all, always keep his voice under control. "What'd you come around here for last night?"

"I don't know." I went over to the window and placed my hands on the sill. I looked down at them with a sense of detachment, as though they were hands somebody had sculptured and put on exhibition somewhere. "I had to." Then I added, with great difficulty, "I thought I belonged here."

I felt him turning to look at me, and so I looked up. He had a particular expression which his face assumed when he understood but didn't think he should show it, a settled, enlightened look; its appearance now was the first decent thing I had seen in a long time.

He suddenly slammed his fist against the suitcase. "I wish to God there wasn't any war."

I looked sharply at him. "What made you say that?"

"I don't know if I can take this with a war on. I don't know."

"If you can take—"

"What good are you in a war with a busted leg!"

"Well you—why there are lots—you can—"

He bent over the suitcase again. "I've been writing to the Army and the Navy and the Marines and the Canadians and everybody else all winter. Did you know that? No, you didn't know that. I used the Post

Office in town for my return address. They all gave me
the same answer after they saw the medical report on
me. The answer was no soap. We can't use you. I also
wrote the Coast Guard, the Merchant Marine, I wrote
to General de Gaulle personally, I also wrote Chiang
Kai-shek, and I was about ready to write somebody in
Russia."

I made an attempt at a grin. "You wouldn't like it in
Russia."

"I'll *hate* it *everywhere* if I'm not in this war! Why
do you think I kept saying there wasn't any war all
winter? I was going to keep on saying it until two seconds after I got a letter from Ottawa or Chungking or
some place saying, 'Yes, you can enlist with us.'" A
look of pleased achievement flickered over his face
momentarily, as though he had really gotten such a
letter. "Then there would have been a war."

"Finny," my voice broke but I went on, "Phineas,
you wouldn't be any good in the war, even if nothing
had happened to your leg."

A look of amazement fell over him. It scared me, but
I knew what I said was important and right, and my
voice found that full tone voices have when they are
expressing something long-felt and long-understood
and released at last. "They'd get you some place at the
front and there'd be a lull in the fighting, and the next
thing anyone knew you'd be over with the Germans or
the Japs, asking if they'd like to field a baseball team
against our side. You'd be sitting in one of their com-
mand posts, teaching them English. Yes, you'd get con-
fused and borrow one of their uniforms, and you'd
lend them one of yours. Sure, that's just what would
happen. You'd get things so scrambled up nobody
would know who to fight any more. You'd make a
mess, a terrible mess, Finny, out of the war."

His face had been struggling to stay calm as he listened to me, but now he was crying but trying to control himself. "It was just some kind of blind impulse you had in the tree there, you didn't know what you were doing. Was that it?"

"Yes, yes, that was it. Oh that was it, but how can you believe that? How can you believe that? I can't even make myself pretend that you could believe that."

"I do, I think I can believe that. I've gotten awfully mad sometimes and almost forgotten what I was doing. I think I believe you, I think I can believe that. Then that was it. Something just seized you. It wasn't anything you really felt against me, it wasn't some kind of hate you've felt all along. It wasn't anything personal."

"No, I don't know how to show you, how can I show you, Finny? Tell me how to show you. It was just some ignorance inside me, some crazy thing inside me, something blind, that's all it was."

He was nodding his head, his jaw tightening and his eyes closed on the tears. "I believe you. It's okay because I understand and I believe you. You've already shown me and I believe you."

The rest of the day passed quickly. Dr. Stanpole had told me in the corridor that he was going to set the bone that afternoon. Come back around 5 o'clock, he had said, when Finny should be coming out of the anaesthesia.

I left the Infirmary and went to my 10:10 class, which was on American history. Mr. Patch-Withers gave us a five-minute written quiz on the "necessary and proper" clause of the Constitution. At 11 o'clock I left that building and crossed the Center Common where a few students were already lounging although it was still a little early in the season for that. I went into the First Building, walked up the stairs where Finny had fallen, and joined my 11:10 class, which was in mathematics. We were given a ten-minute trigonometry problem which appeared to solve itself on my paper.

At 12 I left the First Building, recrossed the Common and went into the Jared Potter Building for lunch. It was a breaded veal cutlet, spinach, mashed potatoes, and prune whip. At the table we discussed whether there was any saltpeter in the mashed potatoes. I defended the negative.

After lunch I walked back to the dormitory with Brinker. He alluded to last night only by asking how Phineas was; I said he seemed to be in good spirits. I went on to my room and read the assigned pages of *Le bourgeois gentilhomme*. At 2:30 I left my room, and walking along one side of the oval Finny had used for my track workouts during the winter, I reached the Far Common and beyond it the gym. I went past the Trophy Room, downstairs into the pungent air of the locker room, changed into gym pants, and spent an hour wrestling. I pinned my opponent once and he pinned me once. Phil Latham showed me an involved method of escape in which you executed a modified somersault over your opponent's back. He started to talk about the accident but I concentrated on the escape method and the subject was dropped. Then I took a shower, dressed, and went back to the dormitory, reread part of *Le bourgeois gentilhomme*, and at 4:45, instead of going to a scheduled meeting of the Commencement Arrangements Committee, on which I had been persuaded to take Brinker's place, I went to the Infirmary.

Dr. Stanpole was not patrolling the corridor as he

habitually did when he was not busy, so I sat down on a bench amid the medical smells and waited. After about ten minutes he came walking rapidly out of his office, his head down and his hands sunk in the pockets of his white smock. He didn't notice me until he was almost past me, and then he stopped short. His eyes met mine carefully, and I said, "Well, how is he, sir?" in a calm voice which, the moment after I had spoken, alarmed me unreasonably.

Dr. Stanpole sat down next to me and put his capable-looking hand on my leg. "This is something I think boys of your generation are going to see a lot of," he said quietly, "and I will have to tell you about it now. Your friend is dead."

He was incomprehensible. I felt an extremely cold chill along my back and neck, that was all. Dr. Stanpole went on talking incomprehensibly. "It was such a simple, clean break. Anyone could have set it. Of course, I didn't send him to Boston. Why should I?"

He seemed to expect an answer from me, so I shook my head and repeated, "Why should you?"

"In the middle of it his heart simply stopped, without warning. I can't explain it. Yes, I can. There is only one explanation. As I was moving the bone some of the marrow must have escaped into his blood stream and gone directly to his heart and stopped it. That's the only possible explanation. The only one. There are risks, there are always risks. An operating room is a place where the risks are just more formal than in other places. An operating room and a war." And I noticed that his self-control was breaking up. "Why did it have to happen to you boys so soon, here at Devon?"

"The marrow of his bone . . ." I repeated aimlessly. This at last penetrated my mind. Phineas had died from the marrow of his bone flowing down his blood stream to his heart.

I did not cry then or ever about Finny. I did not cry even when I stood watching him being lowered into his family's strait-laced burial ground outside of Boston. I could not escape a feeling that this was my own funeral, and you do not cry in that case.

13

The quadrangle surrounding the Far Common was never considered absolutely essential to the Devon School. The essence was elsewhere, in the older, uglier, more comfortable halls enclosing the Center Common. There the School's history had unrolled, the fabled riot scenes and Presidential visits and Civil War musterings, if not in these buildings then in their predecessors on the same site. The upperclassmen and the faculty met there, the budget was compiled there, and there students were expelled. When you said "Devon" to an alumnus ten years after graduation he visualized the Center Common.

The Far Common was different, a gift of the rich lady benefactress. It was Georgian like the rest of the school, and it combined scholasticism with grace in the way which made Devon architecturally interesting. But the bricks had been laid a little too skillfully, and the woodwork was not as brittle and chipped as it should have been. It was not the essence of Devon, and so it was donated, without too serious a wrench, to the war.

The Far Common could be seen from the window of my room, and early in June I stood at the window and watched the war moving in to occupy it. The advance guard which came down the street from the railroad station consisted of a number of Jeeps, being driven with a certain restraint, their gyration-prone wheels inactive on these old ways which offered nothing bumpier than a few cobblestones. I thought the Jeeps looked noticeably uncomfortable from all the power they were not being allowed to use. There is no stage you comprehend better than the one you have just left, and as I watched the Jeeps almost asserting a wish to bounce up the side of Mount Washington at eighty miles an hour instead of rolling along this dull street, they reminded me, in a comical and a poignant way, of adolescents.

Following them there were some heavy trucks painted olive drab, and behind them came the troops. They were not very bellicose-looking; their columns were straggling, their suntan uniforms had gotten rumpled in the train, and they were singing *Roll Out the Barrel.*

"What's that?" Brinker said from behind me, pointing across my shoulder at some open trucks bringing up the rear. "What's in those trucks?"

"They look like sewing machines."

"They *are* sewing machines!"

"I guess a Parachute Riggers' school has to have sewing machines."

"If only Leper had enlisted in the Army Air Force and been assigned to Parachute Riggers' school . . ."

"I don't think it would have made any difference," I said. "Let's not talk about Leper."

"Leper'll be all right. There's nothing like a discharge. Two years after the war's over people will think a Section Eight means a berth on a Pullman car."

"Right. Now do you mind? Why talk about something you can't do anything about?"

"Right."

I had to be right in never talking about what you could not change, and I had to make many people agree that I was right. None of them ever accused me of being responsible for what had happened to Phineas, either because they could not believe it or else because they could not understand it. I would have talked about that, but they would not, and I would not talk about Phineas in any other way.

The Jeeps, troops, and sewing machines were now drawn up next to the Far Common quadrangle. There was some kind of consultation or ceremony under way on the steps of one of the buildings, Veazy Hall. The Headmaster and a few of the senior members of the faculty stood in a group before the door, and a number of Army Air Force officers stood in another group within easy speaking distance of them. Then the Headmaster advanced several steps and enlarged his gestures; he was apparently addressing the troops. Then an officer took his place and spoke longer and louder; we could hear his voice fairly well but not make out the words.

Around them spread a beautiful New England day. Peace lay on Devon like a blessing, the summer's peace, the reprieve, New Hampshire's response to all the cogitation and deadness of winter. There could be no urgency in work during such summers; any parachutes rigged would be no more effective than napkins.

Or perhaps that was only true for me and a few others, our gypsy band of the summer before. Or was it rarer even than that; had Chet and Bobby sensed it then, for instance? Had Leper, despite his trays of snails? I could be certain of only two people, Phineas and myself. So now it might be true only for me.

The company fell out and began scattering through the Far Common. Dormitory windows began to fly open and olive drab blankets were hung over the sills by the dozens to air. The sewing machines were carried with considerable exertion into Veazy Hall.

"Dad's here," said Brinker. "I told him to take his cigar down to the Butt Room. He wants to meet you."

We went downstairs and found Mr. Hadley sitting in one of the lumpy chairs, trying not to look offended by the surroundings. But he stood up and shook my hand with genuine cordiality when we came in. He was a distinguished-looking man, taller than Brinker so that his portliness was not very noticeable. His hair was white, thick, and healthy-looking and his face was healthily pink.

"You boys look fine, fine," he said in his full and cordial voice, "better I would say than those dough-boys—G.I.'s—I saw marching in. And how about their artillery! Sewing machines!"

Brinker slid his fingers into the back pockets of his slacks. "This war's so technical they've got to use all kinds of machines, even sewing machines, don't you think so, Gene?"

"Well," Mr. Hadley went on emphatically, "I can't imagine any man in my time settling for duty on a sewing machine. I can't picture that at all." Then his temper switched tracks and he smiled cordially again. "But then times change, and wars change. But men don't change, do they? You boys are the image of me and my gang in the old days. It does me good to see you. What are you enlisting in, son," he said, meaning me, "the Marines, the Paratroops? There are doggone many exciting things to enlist in these days. There's that bunch they call the Frogmen, underwater demolition stuff. I'd give something to be a kid again with all that to choose from."

"I was going to wait and be drafted," I replied, trying to be polite and answer his question honestly, "but if I did that they might put me straight in the infantry, and that's not only the dirtiest but also the most dangerous branch of all, the worst branch of all. So I've joined the Navy and they're sending me to Pensacola. I'll probably have a lot of training, and I'll never see a foxhole. I hope."

"Foxhole" was still a fairly new term and I wasn't sure Mr. Hadley knew what it meant. But I saw that he didn't care for the sound of what I said. "And then Brinker," I added, "is all set for the Coast Guard, which is good too." Mr. Hadley's scowl deepened, although his experienced face partially masked it.

"You know, Dad," Brinker broke in, "the Coast Guard does some very rough stuff, putting the men on the beaches, all that dangerous amphibious stuff."

His father nodded slightly, looking at the floor, and then said, "You have to do what you think is the right thing, but just make sure it's the right thing in the long run, and not just for the moment. Your war memories will be with you forever, you'll be asked about them thousands of times after the war is over. People will get their respect for you from that—*partly* from that, don't get me wrong—but if you can say that you were up front where there was some real shooting going on, then that will mean a whole lot to you in years to come. I know you boys want to see plenty of action, but don't go around talking too much about being comfortable, and which branch of the service has too much dirt and stuff like that. Now I know you—I feel I know you, Gene, as well as I know Brink here—but other people might misunderstand you. You want to serve, that's all. It's your greatest moment, greatest privilege, to serve your country. We're all proud of you, and we're all—old guys like me—we're all darn jealous of you too."

I could see that Brinker was more embarrassed by this than I was, but I felt it was his responsibility to answer it. "Well, Dad," he mumbled, "we'll do what we have to."

"That's not a very good answer, Brink," he said in a tone struggling to remain reasonable.

"After all that's all we can do."

"You can do more! A lot more. If you want a military record you can be proud of, you'll do a heck of a lot more than just what you have to. Believe me."

Brinker sighed under his breath, his father stiffened, paused, then relaxed with an effort. "Your mother's out in the car. I'd better get back to her. You boys clean up—ah, those shoes," he added reluctantly, in spite of himself, having to, "those shoes, Brink, a little polish? —and we'll see you at the Inn at six."

"Okay, Dad."

His father, left, trailing the faint, unfamiliar, prosperous aroma of his cigar.

"Dad keeps making that speech about serving the country," Brinker said apologetically, "I wish to hell he wouldn't."

"That's all right." I knew that part of friendship consisted in accepting a friend's shortcomings, which sometimes included his parents.

"I'm enlisting," he went on, "I'm going to 'serve' as he puts it, I may even get killed. But I'll be damned if I'll have that Nathan Hale attitude of his about it. It's all that World War I malarkey that gets me. They're all children about that war, did you never notice?" He flopped comfortably into the chair which had been disconcerting his father. "It gives me a pain, personally. I'm not any kind of hero, and neither are you. And neither is the old man, and he never was, and I don't care what he says he almost did at Château-Thierry."

"He's just trying to keep up with the times. He probably feels left out, being too old this time."

"Left out!" Brinker's eyes lighted up. "Left out! He and his crowd are responsible for it! And *we're* going to fight it!"

I had heard this generation-complaint from Brinker before, so often that I finally identified this as the source of his disillusionment during the winter, this generalized, faintly self-pitying resentment against millions of people he did not know. He did know his father, however, and so they were not getting along well now. In a way this was Finny's view, except that naturally he saw it comically, as a huge and intensely practical joke, played by fat and foolish old men bungling away behind the scenes.

I could never agree with either of them. It would have been comfortable, but I could not believe it. Because it seemed clear that wars were not made by generations and their special stupidities, but that wars were made instead by something ignorant in the human heart.

Brinker went upstairs to continue his packing, and I walked over to the gym to clean out my locker. As I crossed the Far Common I saw that it was rapidly becoming unrecognizable, with huge green barrels placed at many strategic points, the ground punctuated by white markers identifying offices and areas, and also certain less tangible things: a kind of snap in the atmosphere, a professional optimism, a conscious maintenance of high morale. I myself had often been happy at Devon, but such times it seemed to me that afternoon were over now. Happiness had disappeared along with rubber, silk, and many other staples, to be replaced by the wartime synthetic, high morale, for the Duration

At the gym a platoon was undressing in the locker room. The best that could be said for them physically was that they looked wiry in their startling sets of underwear, which were the color of moss.

I never talked about Phineas and neither did anyone else; he was, however, present in every moment of every day since Dr. Stanpole had told me. Finny had a vitality which could not be quenched so suddenly, even by the marrow of his bone. That was why I couldn't say anything or listen to anything about him, because he endured so forcefully that what I had to say would have seemed crazy to anyone else—I could not use the past tense, for instance—and what they had to say would be incomprehensible to me. During the time I was with him, Phineas created an atmosphere in which I continued now to live, a way of sizing up the world with erratic and entirely personal reservations, letting its rocklike facts sift through and be accepted only a little at a time, only as much as he could assimilate without a sense of chaos and loss.

No one else I have ever met could do this. All others at some point found something in themselves pitted violently against something in the world around them. With those of my year this point often came when they grasped the fact of the war. When they began to feel that there was this overwhelmingly hostile thing in the world with them, then the simplicity and unity of their characters broke and they were not the same again.

Phineas alone had escaped this. He possessed an extra vigor, a heightened confidence in himself, a serene capacity for affection which saved him. Nothing as he was growing up at home, nothing at Devon, nothing even about the war had broken his harmonious and natural unity. So at last I had.

The parachute riggers sprinted out of the hallway toward the playing fields. From my locker I collected my sneakers, jock strap, and gym pants and then turned away, leaving the door ajar for the first time, forlornly open and abandoned, the locker unlocked. This was more final than the moment when the Headmaster handed me my diploma. My schooling was over now.

I walked down the aisle past the rows of lockers, and instead of turning left toward the exit leading back to my dormitory, I turned right and followed the Army Air Force out onto the playing fields of Devon. A high wooden platform had been erected there and on it stood a barking instructor, giving the rows of men below him calisthenics by the numbers.

This kind of regimentation would fasten itself on me in a few weeks. I no longer had any qualms about that, although I couldn't help being glad that it would not be at Devon, at anywhere like Devon, that I would have that. I had no qualms at all; in fact I could feel now the gathering, glowing sense of sureness in the face of it. I was ready for the war, now that I no longer had any hatred to contribute to it. My fury was gone, I felt it gone, dried up at the source, withered and lifeless. Phineas had absorbed it and taken it with him, and I was rid of it forever.

The P.T. instructor's voice, like a frog's croak amplified a hundred times, blared out the Army's numerals, "Hut! Hew! Hee! Hore!" behind me as I started back toward the dormitory, and my feet of course could not help but begin to fall involuntarily into step with that coarse, compelling voice, which carried to me like an air-raid siren across the fields and commons.

They fell into step then, as they fell into step a few weeks later under the influence of an even louder voice and a stronger sun. Down there I fell into step as well as my nature, Phineas-filled, would allow.

I never killed anybody and I never developed an intense level of hatred for the enemy. Because my war ended before I ever put on a uniform; I was on active duty all my time at school; I killed my enemy there.

Only Phineas never was afraid, only Phineas never hated anyone. Other people experienced this fearful shock somewhere, this sighting of the enemy, and so began an obsessive labor of defense, began to parry the menace they saw facing them by developing a particular frame of mind, "You see," their behavior toward everything and everyone proclaimed, "I am a humble ant, I am nothing, I am not worthy of this menace," or else, like Mr. Ludsbury, "How dare this threaten me, I am much too good for this sort of handling, I shall rise above this," or else, like Quackenbush, strike out at it always and everywhere, or else, like Brinker, develop a careless general resentment against it, or else, like Leper, emerge from a protective cloud of vagueness only to meet it, the horror, face to face, just as he had always feared, and so give up the struggle absolutely.

All of them, all except Phineas, constructed at infinite cost to themselves these Maginot Lines against this enemy they thought they saw across the frontier, this enemy who never attacked that way—if he ever attacked at all; if he was indeed the enemy.

thought it was an impenetrable barrier

false security

ABOUT THE AUTHOR

JOHN KNOWLES, born in Fairmont, West Virginia, was educated at Phillips Exeter Academy and at Yale University. Starting as a newspaper reporter, Mr. Knowles went on to become an associate editor of HOLIDAY. In addition to the William Faulkner Foundation Award, *A SEPARATE PEACE*, his first novel, has won the Rosenthal Award of the National Institute of Arts and Letters and an award from the Independent School Education Board. His third novel, *Indian Summer*, was published in 1966 and was a selection of the Literary Guild. *Phineas*, a collection of short stories, including the one upon which *A SEPARATE PEACE* was based, was published in 1968. Other books by Mr. Knowles include *Morning in Antibes*, *Double Vision* and, most recently, *Peace Breaks Out*. Mr. Knowles has served as a writer-in-residence at Princeton University and at the University of North Carolina, and lectures frequently to university audiences. He makes his home in eastern Long Island.